# THE ABOVE-AVERAGE
# *ADVENTURES*
## OF
# NICHOLAS HERRIMAN

## KEN SHELDON

To the Kids of the
Whipple Free Library!

Ken Sheldon

Cover illustration by Maren Gagne
indeliblemissmaren@gmail.com
*indelibem.crevado.com*

For Tyler and Caleb

# Chapter 1

Nick Herriman was having a bad week. On Monday, he got a D on his geography quiz.

On Tuesday, he tried out for the spring musical, but his voice cracked in the middle of "The Star-Spangled Banner" and his music teacher said, "Maybe next year."

On Wednesday, his best friend Tony Chavez told a joke and Nick laughed so hard that milk squirted out of his nose, right in front of Sarah Williams, the cutest girl in school.

On Thursday, Nick's basketball team—the yellow shirts—lost to the blue shirts, 32 to 4.

That afternoon, as Nick and Tony got off the bus at their corner, Nick said, "I can't believe it. They clobbered us."

Tony shrugged. "You win some, you lose some."

"32 to 4? That's not losing, that's annihilation. You know, just once I'd like to be good at something."

"Hey, you're good at lots of things." Tony said.

"You're a pretty good chess player."

"Are you kidding?"

"OK, you're not a *bad* chess player."

"And I'm definitely not the best chess player."

"That's true. Priscilla Grimes could beat you with one hand tied behind her back." Priscilla Grimes was a skinny girl who didn't have any friends and spent all her time reading or playing chess.

"You're not bad at volleyball," Tony said.

"Not bad, but not great."

"No, not great. Harley Davison--"

"I know," Nick said. "Harley could beat me with one hand tied behind his back."

"Maybe both hands."

Harley Davison was the strongest, most athletic kid at Peabody School. Also the biggest jerk. His real name was Roland, but no one called him that unless they wanted to have free plastic surgery done on their faces.

"Everybody besides me has something they're good at," Nick said, "Like you. You're the funniest person in class."

"That's true," Tony said. "And it's a great responsibility being the class clown. You don't know how many times I've wished I were just an ordinary, unfunny guy. Like you."

"You know, it's amazing," Nick said. "I can be having the worst day of my life, and you always know what to say to make it even worse."

"Hey, what are friends for?"

Then, as if the day hadn't already been bad enough, it was trash day.

Every Thursday, Nick had to take the trash to the dump. (In big cities, trucks came and hauled the trash away, but in Peabody, New Hampshire, everyone took their own trash to the dump.) Going to the dump wouldn't have been so bad if he didn't have to take the trash in his old red wagon, dragging it down the street and praying that no one from school would see him. If they did, his Coolness Quotient would sink from "Below Average" to "So Low You'd Need a Deep-Sea Submarine to Find It."

The only good part about going to the dump was the swap shop, a little building where people brought stuff that was too good to throw away—bicycles that kids had outgrown, old books, stereos with one speaker. The swap shop was so popular that some people came home from the dump with more stuff than they'd brought.

But that day, the pickings at the swap shop were slim: an old pair of skis with no bindings, a table with one wobbly leg, a deflated basketball, boxes of books.

As Nick looked over the junk, a rusted station wagon with fake wood paneling pulled up in front of the swap shop. A man with a thick, dark mustache got out, his belly hanging over his belt like a giant water balloon. He began carrying boxes of stuff into the swap shop. Nick glanced at the boxes and knew right away there was nothing he'd care about. They were full of knickknacks, dishes, pots and pans.

As Nick was checking out an old Monopoly game on the shelves, he heard a loud thunk and turned around. There, in the middle of the swap shop, was a treasure chest.

Well, not exactly a treasure chest. It was a trunk, the kind people had carried on the Titanic—which, if Nick remembered right, were supposedly full of valuables.

The man with the balloon belly walked away, dusting his hands on his pants, and squeezed behind the wheel of the station wagon. In the passenger seat of the car was a white-haired lady, barely tall enough to see out of the window. As the car drove off, she stared back at the boxes in the swap shop as if she were saying goodbye to old friends she was never going to see again.

Nick noticed the vanity plate on the car: IMATALR. He liked figuring out vanity plates, but this one stumped him. After a moment, he gave up and turned back to the trunk.

It was black, with a curved top and dull brass corners. He tried to open the lid, but it was locked, and there wasn't a key in it. He looked in the other boxes, but there was no key in any of them either.

Now what? He had a collection of old keys at home. Maybe one of them would work. But if he went home to get the keys, someone else might take the trunk. He could just take the trunk home, but it looked heavy. What if there were nothing good inside it? Then he'd just have to haul it all the way back. Also, his mother had warned him about bringing home any more junk from the dump.

On the other hand, there was no telling what might be in the trunk—old comic books, a treasure map, jewels—and he'd never know until he opened it up.

He decided to take a chance. He'd just have to sneak it into the house before his mother got home.

It almost worked. He had dragged the trunk halfway up the stairs to his room when he heard the back door open.

His mother appeared at the foot of the stairs. "What is that?"

"A trunk?" he said, as if he weren't quite sure himself.

"Nick, you know what I told you. We have too much junk as it is."

"I know, but—"

"Besides, you have no idea where that thing came from."

Nick's mother was a worrier. She came from a long line of worriers, and she'd gotten worse since his father died. These days, Nick couldn't leave the house without her picturing him being kidnapped or contracting a rare tropical disease.

He had a flash of inspiration. "I thought it would be a good place to put my dirty clothes. You're always telling me not to leave them lying around."

She shook her head. "Nick—"

"Dad would have let me keep it," he said.

That wasn't fair, but it was his last line of defense when he was desperate. And it was true. His dad had let him climb trees, do cannonballs into the lake, and eat snacks that turned your teeth orange.

His mother looked at him for a while and took a deep breath. "All right," she said. "Just make sure it's clean."

"Thanks, Mom!"

He dragged the trunk to his room. Max, his golden retriever, waddled in after him. "Come on, Max. Let's see what's in here."

He pulled out his collection of keys and tried them on the lock. Most of them were too small or the wrong shape. Finally, he found an old skeleton key, the largest one in his collection. He stuck it in the lock and twisted.

Rusty metal scraped against metal. With a thin screech, the lock opened.

# Chapter 2

Nick raised the lid of the trunk. A light coating of dust fell from the edges and a musty smell drifted up from inside.

The smell came from old clothing—shirts, pants, belts, boots—all of which looked as if they hadn't been made in this century. Treasure-wise, this didn't look good.

He dug through the clothes and found a green helmet with odd markings on the sides. The top was dented, as if someone had hit it with a hammer.

He put the helmet on and looked at himself in the mirror. It wobbled on his head like an upside-down mixing bowl—not exactly the latest in protective headgear.

He tossed the helmet aside and kept digging till he came to a pair of running shoes with wings on the sides. He couldn't decide if they were cool or dorky. That was the problem with clothes, you could never tell. Kids had been laughed out of school for wearing the wrong things. At any rate, the shoes looked too big for him. He kept digging.

There were scarves, mismatched gloves and several pieces of rope. He found a pair of red rubber boots and a jeweled belt, odds and ends of jewelry, and a funny round box. Inside the box was a gray businessman's hat, the kind a spy might wear in an old movie. He put the hat on and muttered, "Nick Herriman, Secret Agent."

He kept digging and pulled out vests, handkerchiefs, a red cape, a silky blue bathrobe and an old Indian headdress. Finally, at the bottom of the trunk, was a silver case covered with intricate scrollwork. He snapped it open. Inside was a pair of glasses with a tiny dial between the lenses. "Rats." He closed the case and tossed it aside. He didn't need someone else's old glasses.

There was one more place to check. Along the left side of the trunk was a row of compartments with flaps on top. Nick closed his eyes and whispered "Money, money, money," as he opened the first compartment.

It was filled with pins and fasteners. He lifted the lid of the second compartment. "Jewels. Diamonds. Rubies."

Nope. Thread and yarn.

One more compartment left. He crossed his fingers on both hands. "Gold doubloons. Treasure map."

No such luck. It was buttons. A hundred different shapes, sizes and colors of buttons. So much for treasure.

He tossed the clothes back into the trunk and slammed the lid. All that effort for nothing. Tomorrow, the stupid trunk was going back to the dump.

His mother knocked at the door. "Nick, are you

all right in there?"

"I'm fine, Mom."

"What are you doing?"

"*Nothing.*" He opened the door a crack. "I'm *fine.*"

She saw the hat and gasped. "Oh, my gosh. You look just like your father in that."

Nick didn't know what to say. He knew she missed Dad. Nick missed him too—although after five years he could barely remember what his father looked like. These days, his father was like the hero of an old movie that he used to love but hadn't seen in a long time. "Mom, can't I have any privacy? I didn't want to be disturbed."

A glazed look came over his mother's face. "Must not disturb you," she said in a flat voice.

"Just leave me alone, OK?"

"Leave you alone."

He closed the door. That was weird. He'd never been able to get her off his case that easily. She'd been acting normally until she saw...

The hat. He took it off and studied it closely. For the first time, he noticed a small crescent moon etched into the hatband.

It was crazy. But there was only one way to find out. He ran downstairs. His mother stood pouring noodles into a pot of boiling water.

"Mom, can I go to the dump and bring back a bunch of stuff that might be crawling with germs and termites and cockroaches?"

"What?" She turned to face him. As soon as she

13

saw the hat, the scowl on her face melted away. "Go to the dump," she said blankly. "Bring back a bunch of stuff that might be crawling—"

"Never mind," Nick said, backing out of the kitchen.

He ran back up to his room, breathing hard.

This was incredible—a hat that gave you power over people's minds. He fell back on his bed and stared at the ceiling, imagining what he could do with a hat like this.

*Sarah Williams stopped Nick outside the cafeteria. "Nick," she said breathlessly, "That's such a cool hat."*

*"This?" Nick said, running his finger along the brim. "Glad you like it. Hey, the chess club is having a party after the talent show next Friday. How'd you like to be my guest?"*

*Sarah's eyes went dreamy. "Go to the party with Nick on Friday."*

*"Great," Nick said. "I'll meet you there."*

*Sarah snuggled up next to him. "Oh, Nick." She kissed him on the cheek, a long, slow kiss. Actually, it was more like long, wet slobber.*

Nick's eyes flew open. Max was licking his face.

"Max!" he yelled, jumping up and rubbing the slobber off with a sleeve.

He grabbed a piece of paper and began making a list of things he could do with the hat. First, he'd invite Sarah to the party. Then he'd get himself elected class president. When the annual candy drive came around, he'd sell more boxes than anyone in the history of Peabody School.

Teachers would love him. Girls would worship him. Guys would want to *be* him. Nick Herriman's days as the Most Average Kid at Peabody School were over.

Nick was still thinking of ways to use the hat when he went to bed that night. He fell asleep, and didn't notice a dim blue glow seeping out from under the lid of the trunk.

# Chapter 3

The next day, Tony caught up with Nick as he was headed into the cafeteria. "Hey, cool fedora."

"What?"

Tony pointed to the hat. "That's what they call that kind of hat, a fedora."

"Oh."

"So, are you asking anyone to the chess club party?"

"Yeah, I think so."

"Who?"

"Sarah Williams."

Tony snickered. "Right. And if she's not available, you could ask that girl on the cover of *Sports Illustrated*."

"What do you mean?"

"Look, no offense—you're my best friend and all—but you're not in her league. In fact, I'm not sure you're in the same dimension."

Nick touched a finger to the brim of the fedora. "We'll see."

They went through the lunch line and Nick asked for a hamburger and French fries. "I've been a good boy," he joked with the lunch lady. "You should probably give me some extra fries."

"Give you extra fries," she murmured, piling the plate high.

Nick's grin faded. He'd forgotten about the hat. "Thanks."

Tony followed him into the lunchroom. "Hey, how come she gave you so many fries?"

"I don't know. I guess she likes me."

As they searched for a table, Harley Davison walked past. "Hey, Ridiculous." Harley had nicknames for everyone. Nick was Ridiculous. Tony was Tony Baloney. Priscilla Grimes was Priscilla Gorilla. "Nice hat," Harley said, knocking the fedora off of Nick's head.

The hat hit the floor. Before Nick could pick it up, someone stepped on it. By the time he retrieved the hat, it was battered out of shape. "Idiot," he muttered in Harley's direction, but not loud enough for him to hear.

By this time, Tony had found them seats with Owen Linderman, the shortest kid in seventh grade. Nick tried to unrumple the hat while Owen and Tony talked about a movie they'd just seen. "Remember that scene with the pudding?" Owen said, holding up his tapioca pudding.

Harley appeared behind him and grabbed the pudding. "Thanks, Littleman." Owen's ears burned—he hated being called Littleman. "Tapioca, huh?" Harley said. "Is it true that eating tapioca pudding makes you a wuss?"

Nick glanced around. If that was true, half the kids in the cafeteria were wusses, including some of Harley's best friends. He decided not to mention

17

that.

"What is this stuff, anyway?" Harley asked. "Maggots?"

"Give it back," Nick said.

Harley turned and stared at Nick. "Did you say something, Ridiculous?"

The cafeteria fell silent.

Nick gulped. "Give it back?"

Harley's eyes went blank. "Give it back," he said, and started to hand the pudding back to Owen.

Nick couldn't believe it. Harley was actually listening to him. Then he realized—it wasn't him. It was the hat.

"Wait a minute," Nick said. "Dump the pudding on your head."

Harley hesitated, as if a struggle was going on inside him. "Dump the...pudding...on my head." Slowly, mechanically, his arm went up and turned the bowl over. The pudding landed on his head with a plop.

It was one of the most satisfying moments of Nick's life. The pudding slid down the side of Harley's face and left a large maggoty smear across the front of his jersey.

A low murmur rumbled across the cafeteria. At the next table, a kid lifted his pudding. "Dump the pudding on my head," he mumbled.

Nick looked around. All over the cafeteria, kids were dumping tapioca pudding on their heads.

"Oh, no," he murmured. He could hear the

evening news now...

"Students and teachers at Peabody School were shaken today by another act of seemingly random violence. No one knows what caused Nicholas Herriman to go on a rampage that left hundreds of students with tapioca pudding on their heads.

"He always seemed like such a quiet kid," said fellow student Roland Davison as police hustled Herriman into a squad car.

Tony raised his pudding over his head. "Dump the pudding—"

Nick grabbed his arm. "No, don't do that." He picked up his tray and whispered, "Come on, let's get out of here."

"Let's get out of here," Tony said.

As they dropped their trays off, Tony seemed to snap out of it. "That was weird."

It was worse than weird, Nick thought. It was a disaster. Now he couldn't use the hat to invite Sarah to the party. If he did, he'd end up with a hundred dates.

They left the cafeteria and passed Mr. McCloskey, the school janitor, who was pushing a broom down the hall. Mr. McCloskey always moved at about two miles per year. He had gray hair, a long face and bushy eyebrows. He looked like an old, gray horse. But when he looked at you, it was as if he could see through you, as if he always knew exactly what you were thinking.

Mr. McCloskey glanced at Nick, who felt as if a

metal detector was sweeping over him. It was a look that said, *You're up to something*. And unless Nick was imagining it, Mr. McCloskey was staring at the hat.

For the rest of the day, rumors about the pudding incident flew around the school. Some kids said it was a protest against tapioca. Others thought it was an initiation rite for a secret gang. Even the kids who had been there didn't seem to know what happened.

Except for Harley. He knew exactly what happened. As Nick headed for the bus that afternoon, Harley stopped him and pushed a finger into his shoulder. "I don't know how you did that, Ridiculous. But one of these days, sooner or later— you die."

**Peabody Police Report**
Pudding Disturbance at School
Teachers at Peabody School
reported an incident in which
several hundred students ended
up with tapioca pudding on
their heads. Principal Watkins
had no explanation for the
incident, which he referred to
as "a spontaneous outbreak of
spring fever."

# Chapter 4

The next morning, Nick lay in bed thinking. Yesterday hadn't exactly gone the way he'd planned. If he was going to break out of Averageville—not to mention avoid being killed by Harley—he'd have to figure out what went wrong with the hat and how to use it on one person at a time.

He threw back the covers and jumped out of bed, landing right on his glasses.

"Ow, ow, ow!" He fell back on his bed, rubbing his foot. When the pain eased, he felt around on the floor for his glasses.

They were broken in two pieces.

"Oh, no." His mother was going to kill him. These days, money was always tight. The last thing they needed was to pay for a new pair of glasses.

He tried taping the two halves together, but they kept falling apart. Now what was he going to do? He could barely see without his glasses.

Then he remembered the glasses in the trunk. Maybe they'd work. It was a long shot, but he was desperate. He dug them out and put them on. Suddenly, everything in the room seemed clearer. He looked out the window at a girl walking down the street. She was carrying a book, and as he stared at it, the title seemed to enlarge until he could read it clearly: "Here Come the Arbuthnots."

"Wow." With his old glasses, he couldn't have told she was carrying a book, let alone what the title was.

He noticed an ant crawling along the windowsill. As he looked at it, the ant became giant-sized, with pincers like lobster claws, wiggling feelers, and six hairy legs. "Aaah!"

He jumped back, and the monster-ant shrank into a plain old ant again.

These glasses were incredible. Somehow, they were adjusting for whatever he looked at. The only bad thing about them was the weird dial between the lenses. Maybe he'd tell everyone it was a designer logo. If he was lucky, no one would notice.

They noticed. The minute Nick walked into geography class, Harley Davison said, "Hey, Ridiculous, nice glasses." He leaned close and whispered, "They'll look great on your corpse."

"All right," Mrs. Smelding said. "Take your seats and clear your desks for the quiz."

Nick slid into his seat next to Tony. "Why does she always give quizzes first thing in the morning?"

"The same reason they execute criminals at dawn," Tony said. "So it won't ruin the rest of their day."

"Before we begin, I want to remind you all about the talent show coming up next Friday. Be sure to sign up if you want to participate."

As she began handing out the quizzes, Nick

leaned on his elbow and fiddled with the dial on the glasses. This was sure to be another disaster.

Mrs. Smelding placed a quiz on Nick's desk. "Nicholas, please remove your hat."

He slid the fedora under his chair and stared at the paper. Scrawled across the top was a bright red "D."

He stared at the paper, his cheeks burning. He couldn't believe it—she had given him his grade before he even took the quiz.

All right, he'd show her. He was going to do well on this quiz if it killed him.

1. What is the largest state in the United States?

That was easy. He started to write "California" but stopped. He remembered a joke Tony had told him about Alaska being the biggest state in the country. He wrote Alaska in the blank and saw something flicker at the top of the page.

The D was now a C-.

Nick looked around to see if someone had snuck up and changed the grade. But the other kids were all busy working on their own quizzes. He must have just read it wrong. The next question read:

2. What is the capital of California?
   a. Los Angeles
   b. San Francisco
   c. Sacramento
   d. Fresno

He thought the answer began with an "S" and San Francisco sounded familiar, so he circled "b."

There was another flicker, and the grade at the top of the paper changed back to a D.

Nick frowned and took off the glasses. Maybe they were broken after all.

Or maybe not.

He put the glasses back on, erased his first answer and circled "c" for Sacramento.

The grade changed to a C.

Nick's heart pounded. He glanced over at Audrey O'Malley. Audrey was the smartest kid in their class. She was probably the smartest kid in the western hemisphere—also the most annoying.

Audrey's paper had a grade on it, too. As she wrote an answer on the sheet, the grade flickered from an A to an A-.

Nick looked around at the other kids. They all had grades on their papers, and the grades were changing as they worked on their quizzes.

He took the glasses off and rubbed his eyes. Without them, he could barely even *see* the other kids' papers. But he could tell this much: there was no grade on any of them.

"Nicholas?" Mrs. Smelding snapped. "Is something wrong?"

Nick put the glasses back on and looked down at his paper. "No."

"Then I suggest you keep your eyes on your own paper."

He glanced up at her. Mrs. Smelding was wearing a blue dress. On the wall behind her was a calendar with giant block letters that said, "Monday, May 18."

He peeked over the top of the glasses. Even with his bad eyesight, he could see that Mrs. Smelding was wearing a brown dress, and the calendar read, "Friday, May 15."

There was only one explanation. The glasses were showing him the future.

He worked through the rest of the quiz. After each answer, the grade at the top of the paper went up or down. When it went down, he erased and guessed again. By the time he'd finished, the grade on the paper was an A+.

He leaned back in his chair and stared into space, grinning. For once, he couldn't wait to hand in his paper.

Principal Watkins stood at the podium, smiling from ear to ear. "And now, the moment we've all been waiting for, the award for the All-Time Smartest Student Ever at Peabody School."

A hush fell over the audience as Mr. Watkins opened the envelope. Mrs. Smelding sat on the platform behind him, beaming at Nick, who tried to look humble.

"And the winner is...Nicholas Herriman."

Nick looked up with a "Who, me?" expression as the entire school burst into applause. The other kids pulled him out of his seat and propelled him toward the stage with slaps on his back. As he went up the steps Mrs. Smelding stood, tears forming in her eyes. "Oh, Nicholas," she said. "Nicholas..."

"Nicholas?"

The legs of Nick's chair fell to the floor with a thud. "Huh?"

"If you're done," Mrs. Smelding said, "You may hand in your paper."

Nick looked at his paper. The A+ was still there.

A slow grin spread across his face. Things were about to change. From now on, he was Nicholas Herriman, straight-A student. So long, D+ Dudley. Hello, Boy Genius.

# Chapter 5

At lunchtime, Nick sat by himself—in a place where Harley wouldn't find him—trying to figure out how the glasses worked. He stared at his lunch tray, twisting the dial. Sloppy Joes...fish sticks...sloppy Joes...fish sticks. He'd have to remember to bring his own lunch on Monday. He hated fish sticks.

He pulled out the silver case the glasses came in, hoping it would give him a clue. On the inside cover was a flap. He lifted the flap and a tiny piece of paper fell out.

🕐 knnj rgzqo
🕐 knnj zgdzc
🕐 knnj vzx zgdzc
🕐 knnj sgqntfg

The words looked as if they were written in a foreign language with a serious shortage of vowels—Lower Slobovian or something—with tiny pictures of a clock next to them. He took the glasses off and squinted at the dial. Sure enough, it was a tiny clock, with the big hand fixed at 12.

He twisted the dial to three o'clock. The sloppy Joes turned into fish sticks—it looked as if three o'clock was the future setting.

He turned the dial to six o'clock. As he put the

glasses back on, a woman sat at the table next to him. She had reddish-brown hair that shimmered as it fell to her shoulders. Her eyes were dark brown and she wore a tight red dress. As Nick stared at her, she pulled a sandwich and a book out of a brown paper bag and began to read.

Where had *she* come from? Teachers always ate in the teachers' lounge unless they were on cafeteria duty, and then they were usually yelling at kids for throwing peas. So who was she?

He had a thought and twisted the dial back to the normal setting.

Before his eyes, the woman transformed into Priscilla Grimes, complete with stringy red hair and freckles.

He twisted the dial back to six o'clock. Priscilla morphed back into the beautiful woman.

His mouth hung open. He was seeing Priscilla as she was going to look when she grew up. She was gorgeous. "Wow," he whispered.

She looked over at Nick and smiled. It was an incredible smile, the kind that makes you feel warm all over. He gave her a goofy grin, his heart pounding.

A hand appeared, waving in front of his face. "Hellooo? Earth to Nicholas?"

A tall woman with dark hair pulled into a tight bun stared down at him. "Are you in love or something?"

"Huh?" He looked around. He was surrounded by

grown-up women, all smirking at him.

Panicking, he whipped the glasses off. The women turned into Audrey O'Malley and her friends—blurry, but there was no mistaking that sneer.

"I said, are you in love?" Audrey asked.

"No," Nick said, rubbing his eyes. "I was just...thinking."

"Right," one of the girls said. "Thinking about Priscilla."

They took off, giggling and nudging each other. Nick knew what that meant. By the end of the day, the whole school would think Nicholas Herriman liked Priscilla Grimes. At Peabody School, the Audrey News Network was faster than Twitter.

He slipped the glasses back on, wondering if any of the other kids had seen him staring at Priscilla. Except that there were no other kids. The cafeteria was filled with grownups—grownups who were laughing, throwing food and telling gross jokes that made milk fly out their noses.

He twisted the dial back and forth to see who was who. Some of the kids didn't change much, while others were barely recognizable. Harley Davison became a bald, middle-aged man with a potbelly. Sarah Williams was still cute, young or old.

On the far side of the cafeteria, a pale, skinny man sat down with his lunch tray. His skin was an odd blue-gray color and his eyes seemed to have sunken into his head. What was up with him?

Then he knew. The guy was dead.

30

Nick felt dizzy. He fumbled with the glasses, twisting the dial back quickly. His breath came in gulps and he stared at his lunch tray, forcing himself not to look across the room. He didn't want to know who that kid was.

When his heart stopped pounding, he pulled out the instruction sheet again. There was one more setting he hadn't tried, but he decided to tuck the paper away. Better to leave well enough alone—he didn't want to see anything like that zombie again.

He held out for a whole minute.

He turned the dial to 9 o'clock and put the glasses on. He looked down at the lunch table, but instead, he saw his feet and legs. His lunch tray and the table had disappeared.

He twisted the dial back. The table reappeared.

*Twist.* Table gone. *Twist.* Table back again.

Nick's eyes opened wide behind the thick glasses. X-ray vision!

An idea came to him. He looked around to make sure no one was watching. Then, casually, he looked over at Sarah Williams and twisted the dial to the X-ray setting.

# Chapter 6

At first, Nick wasn't sure what he was seeing. In the middle of Sarah's chest, two misshapen red balloons expanded and contracted. Between them was what looked like a pipe, or maybe a snake that had just eaten—a slimy mass flowed through it toward a sack of fluids that churned like chunky vegetable soup in a washing machine.

Nick turned pale. He was looking at Sarah Williams's guts--and it wasn't a pretty sight.

His own stomach turned as if he was going to throw up. He'd never be able to look at Sarah Williams the same way again. He had to twist the dial back before he puked.

A voice said, "There you are. What are you looking at?"

Nick spun around. A man in a suit and a loud tie was staring at him, his dark hair slicked back over his head. He looked like the host of a late-night talk show, except he was carrying a lunch tray. And his voice didn't sound like an adult's.

"What?" Nick said weakly.

"Never mind," the man said. "I know what you were looking at." He set his tray down. "Come on, shove over."

Nick stared. Who was this guy? The voice sounded familiar, but...

He took the glasses off and squinted at the dial. It was set at six o'clock. He had accidentally spun the dial to the "way future" setting. He set it on normal and put the glasses on again.

It was Tony. Tony, who always talked about becoming a big star someday. And it looked as if he was going to make it.

"Are you OK?" Tony said. "You look sick."

"I'm fine. It's these glasses. They make me a little dizzy."

"They also make you a little dorky."

"Thanks."

"No problem. Hey, are you going to eat that sloppy Joe or are you just holding it hostage?"

Nick slid the tray over to Tony. He was too nervous and excited to eat anyway.

Tony began babbling away, but Nick couldn't pay attention. All he could think about was the hat and the glasses. And the more he thought, the more excited he got. With these things, he could tell the future, see through brick walls, and make people do whatever he wanted. He'd be the smartest, most popular kid to ever walk the halls of Peabody School. And he wouldn't have to worry about Harley anymore. His troubles were over.

Mrs. Smelding and the principal came into the cafeteria, like cops bursting upon a crime scene. They scanned the room, saw Nick, and marched to his table.

"Nicholas," Mr. Watkins said. "Would you come

with us, please?"

OK, so maybe his troubles weren't completely over.

Mr. Watkins leaned over his desk and shook his head. "It's just hard to understand how you could get a perfect score, given your previous record."

Nick glanced at the quiz on the principal's desk. The bright red A+ glared up at him. In a way, Nick couldn't blame Mrs. Smelding for thinking he'd cheated, especially after she'd seen him looking at the other kids' papers. But he really hadn't cheated—at least, not in the way she thought he had.

"Well?" Mrs. Smelding said. "Can you explain it?"

Nick shrugged. "Just lucky, I guess."

"Then you won't mind taking another quiz to demonstrate your luck again."

She pulled out a new quiz and set it on the desk with a pencil. "You will have the same amount of time as before. Principal Watkins will observe while you complete it."

Fifteen minutes later, Mrs. Smelding returned with a smug look on her face. But as she graded the quiz, the smugness faded and a look of confusion replaced it. Her cheeks flushed red as she wrote "B+" at the top of the paper.

"Nicholas, I owe you an apology. Clearly, you studied hard for this quiz. I hope you'll forgive me for misjudging you."

Now Nick turned red. He had purposely gotten a

few questions wrong so it wouldn't look too suspicious. Better safe than sorry. Even Einstein didn't become a genius overnight.

"That's OK," he said. "We all make mistakes."

As he left the principal's office, he passed Mr. McCloskey, who gave him that look again. It was a look that said, *I've got my eye on you.* And this time, Nick was fairly sure—he was staring at the glasses.

# Chapter 7

As soon as he got home, Nick ran up to his room, threw open the trunk and dug through it. Maybe there was something in it to explain the hat and the glasses.

Someone knocked at the back door, then he heard Tony yelling, "Hey, are you home?"

Nick slammed the trunk and covered it with a quilt. Tony was his best friend, but he was also a bigmouth. Until Nick searched the trunk completely, he didn't want anyone else messing with it. He fell on his bed and picked up a comic book.

"How you doing?" Tony said, barging in. "You didn't look so hot at lunchtime. I thought you were going to barf or something." He saw the quilt and yanked it off. "What's this?"

"Just an old trunk," Nick said, peeking over the top of the comic book. "I'm going to clean it out and keep stuff in it."

Tony lifted the lid. "Whew, smelly." He began digging through the clothes. "Whoa, check this out." He held up the green helmet and put it on. "Look, I'm a space alien."

He turned to Nick's window, put his fists on his hips, and yelled, "Beware, feeble earthlings. I am Zobar, conqueror of the galaxy. You must obey me!"

Nick wished he wouldn't stand in the window like

that. Someone might see him and think they were complete idiots.

"Who's going to see us?" Tony said, taking the helmet off. "There's no one out there."

Nick's mouth fell open. "What?"

"I said, there's no one out there, so who's going to see us?" He tossed the helmet on the bed and went back to the trunk.

Nick stared at the helmet. Tony had heard him even though he hadn't said anything out loud!

The helmet rolled off the bed and clunked on the floor. Nick picked it up and put it on as Tony dug through the clothes. He heard Tony say, *There's got to be something good in here or else he wouldn't be hiding it.*

Except that Tony's lips weren't moving.

Tony saw Nick staring at him. "What?"

"Nothing," Nick said. Then he had an idea. "Think of a number."

"Why?"

"Just think of a number."

Tony closed his eyes. Once again, his voice seemed to come from inside Nick's head. *Man, what a grouch. Seven.* He opened his eyes. "Well?"

"Seven?"

"Lucky guess," Tony said. "Try again." He scrunched his eyes tight. This time, Nick heard, *All right, wise guy, try this—*

There was a crackling sound, like static from a radio, and Nick heard, *A red reptilian, two hundred cows then ate onions and sniffed the trees.*

Nick frowned. "What?"

"I didn't say anything."

He jiggled the helmet. "Keep thinking of the number."

Another burst of static crackled across the inside of the helmet, followed by *Eleven million, two hundred thousand, eight hundred and sixty three.*

Nick tried to look as if he was thinking hard. "Seventy-nine?"

"Ha. Not even close."

Nick took the helmet off, his hands trembling. He didn't want to tell Tony that he knew exactly what he'd been thinking.

This was a mind-reading helmet! There was no telling what he could do with it.

*The commentator leaned closer to the microphone and whispered, "We're here at the finals of the world chess championship, pitting the reigning champion--Ivan Nokyurtopov--against a youngster who has only recently burst onto the world chess scene, the amazing Nicholas Herriman."*

*"That's right, Dick. Herriman is a phenomenal player who up until a few months ago was the worst player on his school's chess team."*

*"True, Jane, although he would only have been second-worst if his friend Tony Chavez didn't cheat."*

*"Right. As you know, Herriman never plays without wearing an unusual good luck charm, a bright green helmet."*

*"At this moment, we're waiting for Nokyurtopov to make his next move. Jane, this has clearly been a more difficult match than Nokyurtopov ever expected. It's as if Nick*

*Herriman knows exactly what move his opponent is going to make before he makes it."*

*"He certainly does, Dick. But Nokyurtopov will have to make a move soon because...Wait...Nokyurtopov is moving...he's tipping over his king...he's admitting defeat!*

*"It's incredible, ladies and gentlemen. Twelve year old Nicholas Herriman has beaten the world champion! And the crowd here can't believe it! Listen to them chanting the new winner's name!"*

*"Nick! Nick! Nick!"*

"Nick," Tony said. He waved a hand in front of his face. "Hello? Your mother's home. She's calling you."

"Nick," his mother yelled up the stairs. "It's time to walk Max."

"OK," Nick yelled, hopping off the bed.

Tony let the trunk lid fall with a thud. "What are you doing later?"

Nick's mind raced. He had to get rid of Tony so he could keep exploring the trunk. "I've got homework to do."

"Homework? It's Friday."

"Geography. You know. Got to keep those grades up."

Tony stared at him. "Who are you, and what have you done with my friend Nick?"

"I'll see you later," Nick said, hustling Tony down the stairs.

"It's a clever disguise," Tony yelled, "but we're on to you, alien!"

# Chapter 8

"Come on, Max," Nick said. This was going to be the world's fastest walk—he had more important things to do.

He found Max's leash by the back door, chewed to pieces. "Max! Bad dog."

Max whined and sunk to the floor.

"Yeah, I'll bet you're sorry."

Now what? How could he walk the dog without a leash? He didn't have time for this.

Then he remembered the ropes in the trunk. He ran up to his room and dug them out. One rope was long and worn smooth. A faint smell of sweat and horses rose from it. The other rope was white, about three feet long, with golden thread woven into it—perfect for a temporary leash.

He ran downstairs and tied the rope to Max's collar. "Come on, let's go."

Nick's house sat on a dead-end street. He and Max trotted to the end of the road, where a narrow path led through the bushes to a field. Max had been playing and doing his business in the field since he was a puppy.

He nosed around, searching for the right spot to pee. "Come on," Nick said, anxious to get back to the trunk. "Just pick a spot."

Max finally finished and Nick said, "All right, let's

go. I'll race you home."

Max took off and Nick followed, holding on to the rope. Normally, Nick could keep up with Max, but this time it felt as if Max was dragging him along. He ran faster and faster, picking up speed.

Then, suddenly, Max wasn't running on the ground at all. He was running on air.

Nick stopped and stared, his mouth hanging open. Max kept running, flying around in a circle like a one-dog merry-go-round.

"Max!" Nick shouted, then stopped. What was he supposed to say? Descend? Dive? Come in for a landing?

After a while Max got tired, slowed to a trot and settled back to earth. "Are you OK?" Nick asked.

Max barked happily.

"All right. Let's go home. Slowly."

When they got home, Nick stuck Max in the house, turned around and headed back to the field. He stopped to make sure no one was watching him, took off his belt and slipped the rope through the loops, then tied it in a knot.

"OK, here goes nothing." He took a deep breath and took off across the field.

At first, nothing happened. He ran faster, pumping his arms. He'd almost come to the far side of the field when his feet felt as if they were running on cotton. He looked down.

He wasn't running on anything. The ground was three feet away.

He swung his legs back but kept kicking them as if he was swimming. The harder he kicked, the faster he went. By pointing his arms up or down, he could go higher or lower. There was just one problem.

No matter what he did, he flew a circle, just like Max had. He tried to fly straight, but kept veering to the left, like a grocery cart with a bad wheel.

He experimented with different positions and discovered that, with his right arm tucked back and his left arm forward, he could fly in a nearly straight line. He remembered that superheroes sometimes flew that way in comic books, and now he knew why. Maybe their flying belts needed alignment, too.

He stared down at the ground below as it zipped past. "Cool!" Then he looked up. He was headed right for the trees.

"Aaaaah!" He threw his hands up to protect himself and shot upward, missing the tops of the trees by inches and rocketing into the sky. The field and the houses around it grew smaller every second, and he remembered something from science class about the air being thin way up high. He figured he'd better head back.

He brought his hands down, leveling off. Then he aimed his arms downward.

Instantly, he plunged back toward the earth. Now he was a gold-roped missile heading for the ground—or more specifically, Route 32, the highway that ran past Peabody.

"Whoa-oh-oh!" Nick yelled, the wind shaking his

cheeks. The highway grew closer. He was seconds away from becoming roadkill on Route 32.

At the last moment, he forced his arms up and pulled out of the dive. Now he was flying down the center of the highway, the dotted yellow line flashing below him like an electronic signal. He heard a noise and looked up.

A tractor trailer was headed right for him.

Nick screamed. The truck's horn blared. The truck veered to one side. Nick swerved the other way and barely missed becoming a bugsplat on the truck's grill.

A tall wooden fence ran along the highway. Nick cleared the top of the fence and passed over a backyard, where a woman in a bikini sat by a swimming pool, sunbathing. She saw Nick and screamed.

Nick zipped over yelling, "Sorreeeeee…"

He passed over another fence, into a yard with a clothesline full of washing. He aimed for a space between two towels, then ran into a sheet hanging on the next line. The sheet stretched and the clothesline snapped. Nick shot up into the sky like a kite with a tail made of socks and underpants.

With the sheet wrapped around his head, Nick couldn't see where he was going. He careened around the sky over Peabody, wrestling with the sheet as people on the ground pointed up, their mouths hanging open.

He managed to pull the sheet away from his head,

but the clothesline was still tangled around him. He looked down. There below him was downtown Peabody—the library, Halvorson's market, the bakery, the playground next to the First Church of Peabody...

He looked up. The church steeple was right in front of him.

Nick swerved and missed the spire by inches, but the clothesline caught on its weathervane. He slingshotted back, the clothesline wrapping around the spire like a yo-yo string. With each circuit of the steeple, Nick flew closer to it. In another moment, he would be right on top of it, hanging on for his life.

He gave one great tug and broke free from the clothesline. He shot off, leaving the socks and underwear flapping from the top of the church.

It was time to head home. The sun was beginning to set, and his mother would be frantic, wondering where he was.

He flew back to the field, passing over the street just before his. An old lady came out of a house and began sweeping her porch. She saw Nick, dropped her broom and ran screaming back into the house.

Yes, it was definitely time to head in.

He came in for a landing, then realized he had a problem. He didn't know how to land.

Don't panic, he thought. They do this in the movies all the time.

Right. But how did they do it? To begin with, superheroes always landed on their feet. But that

44

meant getting your legs out in front of you, and how was he supposed to do that?

He flew closer to the ground, slowing down and trying to decide what to do next. At that moment, the sun fell below the trees. Instantly, Nick lost altitude.

It was a rough landing. Nick bounced along, body surfing over dirt and grass like a stone skipping over the surface of a pond. Fortunately, there were no rocks or trees in the way. He came to a stop, face-down in the grass.

"Well," he said, spitting out bits of grass. "That wasn't so bad."

He dusted himself off. As far as he could tell, he hadn't broken anything. He'd taken worse spills off his bicycle. Of course, it was a good thing the rope hadn't quit when he was a hundred feet in the air. He decided not to think about that.

As he ran home, a police car passed by, headed in the direction of the old lady's house. He slowed down, trying not to look like a person who had just been buzzing around town terrorizing old ladies.

His mother was waiting for him by the back door. "Where have you been? I was just about to call the police. I thought you were..." She stopped. "Nick, what have you been doing?"

He looked down at himself. The front of his shirt and pants were streaked with dirt and grass stains. His sneakers were caked in dirt.

"Some kids and I were playing baseball," he said, holding the rope behind his back." I had to steal home."

"Nick, you've got to be more careful. You could break a bone doing that. And the next time you take off without telling me, you're grounded."

Grounded, Nick thought. Right.

**Peabody Police Report**
Suspicious flying object.
Residents of Peabody reported an unusual object that was seen flying over the town on Friday. Eyewitnesses reported seeing a bird, a plane or a UFO. Police are investigating.

# Chapter 9

Nick ran up to his room and threw open the trunk. First the hat, then the glasses, now the rope. Was everything in the trunk magic?

The shiny blue bathrobe lay on top. He slipped it on.

Nothing happened. He looked in the mirror to see if he'd grown taller or become invisible. But he was still just Nick, wearing a weird blue bathrobe.

Maybe the robe made you super smart. "What is the capital of South Africa?"

The mirror-Nick shrugged. He didn't know either.

All right, maybe everything in the trunk wasn't magic.

He pulled everything out again, paying closer attention this time. Some of the clothes didn't fit him, and others looked so weird that he couldn't imagine wearing them even if they did give him magic powers.

One thing that did fit was a silky purple shirt. One arm had a tear along the seam, and the buttons were on the wrong side, but otherwise it fit him fine. He put on the red cape, stuck the Indian headdress on his head, wrapped the Oriental scarf around his waist, and pulled on the red rubber boots. "Ta-da!"

He looked like the winner of the World's Weirdest Halloween Costume.

"Maybe not."

He took off the headdress and scarf. As he did, Max wandered into the room and hopped up on the bed.

"Max, how many times do I have to tell you not to jump on my bed?" He heard a faint click. "Now get off," he said, and stomped his foot.

The next thing Nick knew, he was headed for the ceiling. It was as if his floor had become the world's springiest trampoline.

He threw his arms up to protect his head as he crashed against the ceiling.

Max dove for cover under the bed. Nick tumbled down, landed on his toes, and bounced again.

He looked down. It was the boots.

Now he was headed for the bedroom wall. His shoulder hit the wall and he glanced off, hit the ceiling again, and bounced backwards this time.

As he flew past his bed, he grabbed one of the bedposts and hung on, spinning around like a tetherball on a pole.

He spun around a few times, gradually slowing down until his feet touched the ground. They bounced again, but Nick held tight to the bedpost until the boots settled down, like a rubber ball losing its bounce.

"Nicky, what's going on up there?" his mother yelled up the stairs. "Are you jumping on the bed?"

"No. I just...dropped something."

"Well, be careful."

Nick stared at the boots. This was incredible—anti-gravity boots! With these, he could become the champion high-jumper of all time. He'd be Nick "Rebound" Herriman on the basketball court. He could leap tall buildings in a single bound.

Of course, he'd have to figure out how to turn them on and off first. Until he did that, the chances of killing himself were also pretty good.

He lay back on his bed and stuck his feet in the air, like a bug on its back, then pulled the boots off and set them down carefully.

Max whined from under the bed.

"It's OK, Max. You can come out now."

But Max was wedged under the bed and didn't seem anxious to come out.

"Come on," Nick said, laying on the floor and grabbing the side of the bed. "Get out of there."

The bed rose in the air as if it were made out of Styrofoam.

Max looked at the bed hovering over him and decided maybe it was time to leave after all. He darted out of the room and Nick gently put the bed back down.

Now what was going on? He had taken everything else off except for the purple shirt.

The purple shirt.

He lifted the bed again. It was about as heavy as a jelly donut.

He tried lifting it with his other arm. The bed didn't budge.

It had to be the rip in the sleeve. Somehow, it was causing a malfunction on that side. Still, having super-strength could come in handy, even if it was only on one side.

He went back to the trunk and pulled out a bunch of belts. One of them was black, with colored jewels set into it: red, orange, yellow, green, light blue, dark blue and purple, all lined up across the front like a rainbow.

He wrapped the belt around his waist—it was made of rubber, so it stretched to fit him perfectly. As he connected the buckle in the front, his hand hit one of the jewels and he heard a faint sound, like a bell dinging.

The room spun around and Nick felt as if he was going to faint. But he didn't. Instead, he started to grow.

And grow. And grow. Six feet. Eight feet, ten, twelve, fourteen feet.

By the time Nick stopped growing, he was scrunched up against the ceiling of his bedroom, barely able to move.

Max came back into the room, saw Nick, and barked anxiously.

"MAX, IT'S ME," Nick boomed, his voice sounding like a clap of thunder.

Max backed away, whimpering.

"IT'S OK, MAX," Nick whispered. "RELAX."

Nick's mother yelled, "Nick, what are you doing up there? Are you OK?"

"I'M...FINE," Nick said as quietly as possible, though he still sounded like a tugboat horn.

"Well, turn that radio down. You're shaking the whole house!"

Nick tried to stay calm. If pressing one of the jewels had made him into a giant, pressing a different one should make him normal again. But which one?

He twisted his head to look at the belt, which wasn't easy, pressed up against the ceiling. The jewel he'd hit was on the right side, so maybe one of the ones on the left side would fix things.

He inched his arm down slowly and pressed the red jewel.

There was another ding, the room spun again, and Nick felt himself falling. It was like being on the Tower of Doom ride at the state fair.

He landed on his bed and kept falling. His bed seemed to shoot out in all directions until it was the size of a soccer field.

He stood up. The bedposts were like giant trees at the four corners of the bed. The ceiling was miles away.

OK, he thought. The red jewel was the wrong one. But if the buttons went in order, one of the middle ones should make him normal-sized again— unless of course it made him microscopic, or so big that he wrecked the house.

As he decided which button to press, an earthquake shook the bed. He looked up as two immense paws landed on the edge of the bed.

Looming between them was the gigantic head of Max.

"Max, go away!" Nick yelled. Except that to Max, he sounded like a cricket chirping.

Max panted, his warm breath washing over Nick. Nick thought he was going to throw up. It was like being downwind of a colossal garbage truck.

Max leaned closer and sniffed. A giant, sucking wind blew past Nick and into Max's enormous nostrils.

"Stop it, Max!" Nick squeaked.

Max opened his mouth stuck his tongue out.

"Max! No!" Nick screamed.

It was too late. Max's tongue scooped him up like a bug on an enormous, slimy rug.

# Chapter 10

This was the worst disaster yet. Nick was about to become a puppy treat for his own dog. A mutt morsel. A canine canapé.

He reached for the belt and pressed the first button he could find. No matter what happened, it had to be better than being inside Max's stomach.

The belt dinged.

In an instant, Nick was the size of a toy soldier. In two instants, he was as big as an action figure. Three instants and he was hamster-sized. That's when he fell out of Max's mouth.

He kept growing, and when he finally stopped growing, he stood up.

Max stared at him. They were eye to eye.

"Great," Nick said. "I'm a midget." He hadn't been this size since Max was a puppy.

Max barked happily and licked his face.

"Back off, Max." He wasn't ready to forgive Max for almost eating him.

This time, he studied the belt closely before pressing anything. The jewels on the right side had made him larger and the ones on the left had shrunk him, so he figured the green one in the middle should be the one for normal size.

He pressed it.

Nothing happened.

He pressed it again.

No ding. No spinning room. And Nick was still a midget.

"Oh, no." Of all the sizes to be stuck in, this was the worst. He'd be the laughingstock of Peabody School. They'd probably stick him back in first grade.

He was too upset to be cautious now. He pressed the light blue button, the belt dinged, and Nick shot up till his head touched the ceiling.

That was better, but he couldn't stay that way. He'd heard of people growing overnight, but not four feet.

He tried the green button again. Still nothing.

Then he had a thought. He undid the belt buckle and got ready to take it off.

He pressed the yellow button, heard the ding, and started to shrink. When he was close to his normal size, he whipped the belt off.

He looked at himself in the mirror. Too tall by several inches. He didn't mind being a little taller, but that much might be hard to explain.

He put the belt back on and tried again. This time he was too short by a few inches.

After several minutes of growing and shrinking, Nick managed to get back to his normal height. Then he folded the belt carefully and put it aside. That was another item that would have to wait until he figured out how to use it.

He went back to the trunk, still searching for some explanation for all the incredible things in it. He went through the side compartments, emptying them out completely. As he did, he noticed that the bottom of the last compartment was higher than the others.

He ran his hand around the inside and felt a button on one side. He pressed it, and the bottom of the compartment flipped up.

Inside, he found a pocket watch, a gold medallion, and an odd crystal.

The watch was old-fashioned and tarnished, the kind train conductors carried. Engraved on the cover were planets spinning around a sun. It was a map of the solar system.

He wound the stem and pried open the watch cover. The watch ticked and the second hand swept slowly around the face. "Awesome."

He stuffed the watch into his pocket and examined the medallion, which had a gold chain attached to it. In the middle of the medallion was an engraving of an owl, with writing around the outside: Gnosis - Aoratos – Metamorfosi – Anoixis.

On a hunch, he gripped the medallion tightly and closed his eyes. I wish I had a million dollars.

He opened his eyes and looked around. Nothing. He went to his dresser and pulled out his wallet to see if a million dollars had appeared in it.

Nope. He found his bank book. It showed thirty-seven dollars and fifteen cents, just like always. If this medallion was magic, it apparently didn't include delivery.

He put the medallion aside and studied the crystal.

It was cloudy-clear, like quartz, but it had a dark blue center, almost as if it had been wrapped around something. As he gazed at the crystal, it vibrated in his hand.

"Whoa," he yelled, dropping it back into the secret compartment. It landed on a yellow lined sheet of paper, folded in quarters. He unfolded the paper.

| btrsnldq | hsdl | edzstqdr | oqnakdl |
|---|---|---|---|
| Ldmszkn | gdklds | qdzc lhmcr | cdmsdc, lzjdr lhrszjdr |
| Jhc Bnlds | vhmfdc rgndr | rtodq roddc | roddc bnmsqnk oqnakdl |
| Dk Chzakn | lzfhb qnod | nadxr bnllzmcr | nmkx nadxr Rozmhrg |
| Bzoszhm Vnmcdq | qnod adks | ekxhmf | kdzmr sn kdcs, ezhkr zs rtmcnvm |
| Lhrr Lhqzbkd | otqokd akntrd | rtodq rsqdmfsg | qdozhq rokhs rdzl |
| Sgd Rgzcd | edcnqz | lhmc bnmsqnk | qdrgzod |
| Dkkdm Jmhfgs, OH | rbzqe | hmuhrhah khsx | qdozhq qtm |
| Bgqnmnr | onbjdsvzsbg | rsnor shld? | rsdl rshbjr |
| KNRS ZMC ENTMC: | | | |
| ? | fkzrrdr | | |
| Sgd Dmbgzmsdq? | ldczkkhnm | | CZMFDQ: JDX SN SGD FZSD |
| ? | rsnmd | | |
| ? | idvdkdc adks | | |
| ? | qzchn? | | |

It was a list of some kind, written in the same

weird language as the instruction sheet for the glasses. How was he supposed to read that?

He thought about showing it to his mother, but she probably wouldn't be able to read it either. It might also make her ask questions about the trunk. And he couldn't think of anyone else he could trust.

He folded the paper and tucked it into his pocket. Something told him this was the key to the secrets of the trunk. When he figured out how to read it, he wouldn't be simply the most popular kid at Peabody School.

Nick Herriman would be the smartest, strongest, most popular kid in the whole world.

# Chapter 11

Nick woke up early on Saturday morning, pulled the clothes out of the trunk and sat with the yellow sheet, trying to translate it.

Max scratched at the door until Nick let him in. "All right," he said. "But don't chew on anything."

He closed the door again as Max sniffed at the clothes. He stuck his nose under the green helmet, which gave Nick an idea. Why not?

He strapped the helmet on and stared into Max's eyes. "Max, what are you thinking?"

A deep, goofy voice inside his head said, *Eat? Eat?*

A chill ran down Nick's spine. It worked. He could read animals' minds!

Max stood up, his tail wagging. *Eat? Eat, eat, eat?*

"No, Max," Nick said. His heart pounded. "It's not time to eat."

Max looked disappointed. *Trout?*

"Trout? What does that mean? You want fish?"

Max barked at the door. Trout! Trout, trout, trout!

"Oh, out." Nick slapped the helmet and a burst of static crackled.

Out, out, out, out! Max barked.

"No, Max, we're not going out." He stared into Max's eyes again. "Tell me what it's like being a dog."

Max cocked his head. *Eat?*

"No, it's not time to eat."

Max's tail slumped. He collapsed on his paws and looked up at Nick with big eyes. *Eat?*

Nick sighed. This wasn't working as well as he'd hoped. Just because you could understand animals didn't mean they had anything important to say.

He had another idea, and put on the fedora. As long as there weren't a lot of other people—or dogs—around, he figured he couldn't get into trouble with it.

"Max," he said, staring into his eyes. "Play dead."

Max jumped up and licked his face.

"No, Max, dead. Play dead."

Max barked.

"Never mind." Clearly, there wasn't enough gray matter between Max's ears to be affected by the hat.

Downstairs, the back door opened and he heard Tony talking to his mother.

"He's upstairs," his mother said. "Go on up."

Nick stuffed the clothes back into the trunk along with the yellow sheet. He grabbed the crystal from his dresser and stuck it in his pocket—he didn't need Tony asking questions about that, either.

Tony burst in and headed straight for the trunk. "Hey, what's happening? You still wearing that hat? Is there anything in here I can wear?"

"No," Nick said. "I mean..." His mind raced. Now he *really* didn't want Tony messing around with the trunk. He grabbed his skateboard. "Come on, let's go to the park."

Tony stopped in his tracks and said slowly, "Let's

go to the park."

Nick wondered why Tony was suddenly being so agreeable until he saw himself in his mirror, wearing the fedora. He grinned, wishing he'd had it a long time ago. It would have made life with Tony a lot easier.

Yates Park was in the center of town. By the time they got there, Tony had snapped out of his trance and was telling a joke about a farmer and a donkey. "So the farmer says—"

A station wagon with fake wood sides drove by and Nick caught a glimpse of its license plate: IMATALR.

"That's it!" he yelled.

"What?"

Nick pointed toward the car as it turned a corner. "That's the car!"

"What car?"

"The car from the dump."

"What?"

"Never mind," Nick said. "Come on."

Tony's face went blank. "Come on," he said, and followed after Nick like a robot learning to run for the first time.

By the time they got to the corner, the station wagon was several blocks away. Nick pushed the glasses up on his nose and stared at the license plate. "I...M...A...T...A...L...R."

"You're a what?" Tony said sleepily.

"That's the license plate. I,M,A,T,A,L,R."

Tony squinted down the street. "You can see that?"

"Sort of." He didn't want to let Tony know how good the glasses were.

"So what does it stand for?"

"I don't know. I was just curious." Maybe IMATALR was the same language as the list from the trunk. And just maybe, the guy who dropped off the trunk could translate the list.

"Why don't you ask the police?" Tony said. He pointed to the Peabody police station across the street. "They could look it up on their computer so you could ask the owner."

"Oh, right. I'm sure they'd be happy to..." Nick stopped. Maybe they *would* be willing to help him.

He adjusted the fedora and looked Tony in the eyes. "Why don't you just wait here for me?"

Tony went glassy-eyed. "Wait here for you."

"Great. I'll be right back."

*Nick Herriman, Private Eye, walked into the Peabody Police Department, shaking the rain from his hat like bullets off a tin roof. The department wasn't much to look at, a hole-in-the-wall operation with one patrolman sitting behind a plate glass window. That was good. Herriman didn't like having a lot of people around when he was on the job.*

*The cop was a young guy with a crew cut and an attitude. He looked up as Nick stepped in off the street. "Oh, it's you, Herriman. What's the matter, did you run out of low-life punks to hang out with?"*

"Yeah," Nick said, his eyebrows arched. "That's why I came here."

*The cop turned red.* "Yeah? Well, there's only one thing I have to say to you."

*Nick leaned back against the counter, took off his hat and fixed the crease.* "And what would that be?"

"Can I help you?"

Nick looked up quickly. "What?"

"Can I help you?" the officer repeated.

"Oh. I need to find out who a license plate belongs to. Can you look it up for me?"

The officer shook his head. "Sorry. Can't do it. Unless of course you have a court order."

"How do I get one of those?"

"You don't. Sorry." He kept typing on the computer.

A pencil and pad of paper lay on the counter. Nick wrote the letters IMATALR on the pad. Then he put the hat on and slid the paper under the glass. "Are you sure you can't look this up for me?"

The officer glanced up with an annoyed look, a look that melted away as soon as he saw the hat.

"Look up license plate," the officer said. He typed the query into his computer. A moment later, a piece of paper clattered out of the printer and he handed it to Nick.

"Thanks very much," Nick said, folding the paper and slipping it into his back pocket. He turned to leave, then said, "Oh. You probably don't want to tell anyone else about this, OK? In fact, you should forget I was even here."

"Forget you were even here," the officer said.

Nick left the station. Tony looked up and shook his head as if he were waking up from a nap. "Any luck?"

"No problem," Nick said, running a finger along the brim of the hat. "You just have to know how to ask."

He glanced at the paper the police officer had given him.

SEARCH RESULTS
NAME:            PLINSKI, NATHAN
PLATE NUMBER:    IMATALR
ADDRESS:         141 MAIN ST, ELM CITY

Nick groaned. Elm City? That was miles away. How was he supposed to get there? His mother would never let him ride his bike that far. And she wouldn't drive him there unless he had a good reason.

Or would she?

"Come on," Nick said, grabbing Tony by the arm. "I've got a better idea than skateboarding."

"Come on," Tony said, glassy-eyed.

# Chapter 12

Nick opened the back door and yelled, "Mom?"

There was no answer. Where had she gone to?

A magazine lay open on the kitchen table. It showed a woman in combat gear, pointing a chemical sprayer at a patch of green slime growing in her shower stall. The article's headline was, "Mold: the Silent Invader Threatening Your Family!"

Nick's mother had underlined a sentence in the article: "Toxic mold can lurk in damp cellars, under the eaves of leaky roofs, even in piles of old clothes." The words "old clothes" were underlined three times.

He began to get a bad feeling about this.

He ran upstairs to his room muttering, "Please, please, please," and threw open the door.

The trunk was still there. He breathed a sigh of relief as he knelt in front of it and opened the lid.

It was empty.

"No!"

A faint smell of bleach rose from inside. This had his mother's antifungal fingerprints all over it.

Tony ran up the stairs, "What's going on?"

Nick raced past him. "Never mind." He ran to the kitchen wastebasket under the sink. It was empty.

He checked all the other wastebaskets, including the garbage can out back. There was no sign of the clothes.

Just then, his mother's car pulled into the driveway. Nick ran out yelling, "Mom! What did you do?"

"Relax, Nick," she said, getting out of the car. "I didn't do anything."

"But where are all the—"

She opened the back door and pulled out a laundry basket. "I took them to the laundromat. Don't worry, I know how much you love your dress-up box."

Nick's ears burned. "It's not a dress-up box!"

"All right, your costume box. Anyway, since you're determined to keep this stuff, I decided to wash it."

"What?"

She handed the basket to him. "I also cleaned out the trunk, so now you can put this stuff back."

Nick carried the basket into the house, barging past Tony. "Wait here."

"Wait here," Tony mumbled.

Up in his room, Nick emptied the laundry basket into the trunk. Everything seemed to be there, and it didn't look as if she had found the secret compartment. He'd have to check everything over later to make sure it still worked OK.

When he came downstairs, his mother was looking over his geography quiz. "Nick, this is wonderful. Your father would be so proud."

Nick didn't feel like discussing his sudden knowledge of mountains, rivers, and state capitals.

"Can Tony and I go to—"

"Your father always had a terrible time with geography. He would make the silliest mistakes. Once, he referred to Mexico as Texaco. Another time, he talked about visiting the U.S. capital in Philadelphia. I said, 'That would be hard, since they moved it to Washington, D.C., in 1800.' He got an odd look on his face and said, 'Oh, right.' Isn't that funny?"

Funny? It was pitiful, Nick thought. Even he wasn't that bad at geography. "So, can you take us to the movies in Elm City?"

"Not today. I've got too much work to do."

"Please," he said, waiting for her to look at him and adjusting the hat slightly. "I really need to go to Elm City."

She looked at him in the mirror over her desk and an odd expression came over her face. After a moment she said, "I'm sorry, but I've got too much to do."

Nick slammed the back door on the way out. "Rats." First the stupid hat affected everyone, then it wouldn't work at all. Now how was he supposed to get to Elm City?

Tony seemed to be coming around. "What's up?" he asked.

"Nothing. I wanted to go to town, but—"

The back door opened and Nick's mother looked out. "Nick, I just had an idea. How would you guys like to go to the movies in Elm City?"

67

Nick stared at her and grinned. "Sure." A delayed reaction was better than none.

# Chapter 13

At one time, Elm City had been a thriving metropolis full of stores and shoppers. But these days, everyone shopped at the mall outside of town. Main Street looked like a scene from an old movie, with big brick buildings full of empty storefronts and businesses that sold stuff you couldn't imagine anyone wanting to buy.

Nick's mother dropped him and Tony off on Main Street near the movie theater. "I'll pick you up right here in two hours," she said.

As soon as she drove off, Nick started walking in the opposite direction from the theater.

"Where are you going?" Tony said.

Nick lowered the hat brim and whispered, "I've got to go check something out first. You just wait here, OK?"

Tony's eyes glazed over. "Just wait here."

Nick took off, glancing at the paper the policeman had given him. 141 Main Street would be a few blocks away. He counted off the buildings: 117...125...133...

His pocket felt warm and he reached in. The crystal was giving off heat. It almost seemed to be saying, *You're getting closer.*

He found 141 Main Street, a brick building with a small store on the street level. A sign above the door read "Plinski and Son, Tailors."

Nick stared at the sign. *IMATALR*. "I'm a tailor," he whispered.

He tried the door, but it was locked. Then he noticed a small card stuck in the glass.

Out of business.

"Rats." Now how was he supposed to talk to Mr. Plinski?

Next door was a cigar store and news shop. The man behind the counter was smoking a large cigar and reading the newspaper as Nick walked in.

"Excuse me," Nick said. "Can you tell me what happened to Mr. Plinski?"

The man squinted at Nick through a haze of smoke. "Nate? He had a stroke. Had to close the shop."

"What about his son?"

The man snickered. "Son? Mister 'I'm-too-good-for-my-old-man's-business?' That son? Like he should care his old man has a stroke and can't keep up with the work." He pointed the cigar at Nick. "No, better he should stick the old man in a nursing home and make his mother move out of her home, the only home she's known for forty years."

"Mr. Plinski's in a nursing home?" The guy from the dump didn't seem that old.

"Yeah," the man said and went back to reading his paper. "Beth Israel or something like that. Over in Peabody. Where his nudnik son lives."

That explained it. The fat guy was Mr. Plinski's son. And he lived in Peabody, where Nick lived. Where he had just come from.

"Thanks," he said, and headed back to where he'd left Tony. As he passed the tailor shop, he didn't notice that the door was slightly ajar now. Nor did he see the figure in the alley next to the shop—a tall person in a black hat and long, dark coat who stood in the shadows staring at everyone who passed by.

The movie lasted for two hours—Nick checked his watch every few minutes to see when it would be over. He couldn't wait to find Mr. Plinski and ask him about the trunk.

When the movie finally ended, Nick and Tony left through the back exit, which emptied onto a side street.

"That was great," Tony said. "I loved the part where the fire hydrant exploded."

"Yeah," Nick said absent-mindedly. He stuck his hand in his pocket. As he did, the crystal shook violently, as if there were a rattlesnake inside that wanted to get out. Nick yanked his hand out of his pocket.

Tony pretended to be talking on a cell phone. "Hello, Nick? Are you there?" He stared at the imaginary phone. "Huh. No signal."

"Sorry," Nick said. "I was thinking about something."

"Are you OK? You've been acting strange lately,

you know that?"

"I'm fine."

Across the street from the theater, a tall figure in a dark coat stood in the shadows, his hat pulled down over his eyes. He raised his right hand and pointed at the theater. On the hand was a red ring with a lightning insignia.

# Chapter 14

As soon as they arrived home, Nick got rid of Tony and told his mother he was going out again.

He started running toward the only nursing home in Peabody he knew about. It was called Beth Geber—he wasn't sure why anyone would name a nursing home after a girl, but he figured that had to be the place the man in the tobacco shop meant.

When he got there, he knew it was the right place. There, parked in front, was the station wagon with the IMATALR license plate.

He walked through the front door and stopped. Coming down the hallway toward him was the fat man with the mustache from the dump, and holding on to his arm was the old lady.

"He looks terrible," the lady said. "They're not feeding him right."

"He's fine," the man said.

Nick took off the fedora and turned his back, pretending to be looking at a painting on the wall. There was something about the younger Mr. Plinski that he didn't trust. "They're feeding him what the doctor ordered," he said.

"Doctor, schmocter," Mrs. Plinski said. "I've been feeding Nathan Plinski for 40 years. Doctors should know how to feed him better?"

They left, still arguing, and Nick found a desk with

a nurse sitting behind it.

"Can I visit Mr. Plinski?"

"Of course. You'll just have to sign in." She slid a book toward him. "Mr. Plinski's very popular today."

Nick signed the book, glancing at the line just above his. *Joseph and Eva Plinski, Paradise Lane, Peabody.* Next to that, under a column labeled "Relationship to patient," it said "*son, wife.*"

Nick wrote down his address and put "friend" — at least, he hoped Mr. Plinski would think he was a friend.

"Mr. Plinski is in Room 27," the nurse said. "But I have to warn you, he's a little confused today."

*Confused about what?* Nick wondered. He found Room 27 and stood outside it for a moment, not sure what to expect.

He walked in. Mr. Plinski sat in a chair by the window, a tiny man with wrinkled skin, bald except for tufts of gray hair above his ears. He was playing with the hem of his bathrobe but looked up as Nick appeared in the door.

"Come in, come in," he said, a smile spreading across his face. "Sit."

Nick pulled up a chair and Mr. Plinski whispered, "Are they gone?"

"Who?"

He nodded toward the door. "The old lady and that nudnik with the mustache."

He didn't recognize his own wife and son. So that's what the nurse meant by confused. "Yeah,"

Nick said. "They're gone."

"Good. Can't stand those people. Always asking crazy questions. What year is it? Who's the president?" He leaned closer to Nick. "How did you get in?"

Nick shrugged. "I just asked if I could see you."

Mr. Plinski glanced at the fedora in Nick's hands, then slapped his forehead. "Of course. Such a schlemiel I am. Like *you* would have trouble talking your way in."

What did that mean? Then he realized—Mr. Plinski thought he was the owner of the hat. "Actually, I—"

"Don't tell me, I know. It's on the blink again."

"What?"

"Let me see it," Mr. Plinski said, reaching for the hat. "Remember the first time you brought it in? I told you I'd do what I could, but I made no promises. A hat like this was not meant for sitting on. Other hats, maybe, but not this one."

As Mr. Plinski spoke, he worked with the hat, smoothing it between his gnarled fingers, reshaping the crown and the brim. "This hat is one in a million. So what does he do? He sits on it, ladies and gentlemen. He falls out of windows and lands on it. He gets into fights with Dr. Bad-Breath or the Kidney Crusher. Then he wonders why it doesn't work right anymore and he wants me to fix it."

"No, it works fine," Nick said. "Well, actually, sometimes it—"

"All right, all right," Mr. Plinski said, raising a hand. "No charge."

"What?"

"No charge." He handed the hat back to Nick. It looked like new. "You're not happy with my work, there's no charge. That's Nathan Plinski's motto, has been for forty years. And do I have a lack of customers? Do you see me begging for work?" He swept his hand around the room as if it were crowded with customers.

Nick hesitated. "Mr. Plinski, can I ask you a question?"

"Can he ask me a question, he says? Like I'm so busy I don't have time to answer a question for one of my oldest and best customers? So ask."

"Mr. Plinski, who am I?"

Mr. Plinski eyed him suspiciously. "You don't know who you are?"

"Sure, but—"

"Ah. I get it. You want to see if I'll tell anyone *else* who you are. After what, twenty years, you don't trust me anymore? You think I'm going to shoot my mouth off to everyone who comes into the shop that I do work for Mr. Mack Morris, also known as the mysterious..."

Nick leaned closer, but Mr. Plinski just raised a finger in the air. "No, my lips are sealed."

That gave Nick an idea. He put the fedora on.

"And don't go trying the hat on me," Mr. Plinski said, closing his eyes. "I won't look at you."

OK, Nick thought. He'd try a different approach. He removed the hat and said, "Mr. Plinski, you know that trunk of yours?"

The old man opened his eyes narrowly. "What about it?"

"Is there anything...special about it?"

Mr. Plinski held his hand to his chest as if the question gave him heartburn. "Again with the questions."

"I'm sorry. I just wondered—"

"No, no, it's OK. You're a man with secrets. But you're not the only one, you know. Other people have secrets too." He tapped Nick's chest with a bony finger. "And I guard them all. Nathan Plinski knows how to maintain a confidence, believe me. The secrets of the trunk are safe with me."

Nick didn't want them to be safe with him. He pulled out the yellow sheet of paper. "What about this? Does it look familiar?"

Mr. Plinski glanced at the paper. "No. I never saw that paper before in my life. Especially I never saw that paper."

"But I found it in the trunk—"

Mr. Plinski shook his head and patted Nick's knee. "Not to worry, my friend. I told you, my lips are sealed."

Nick tried to think of a way to unseal Mr. Plinski's lips. But while he was thinking, the old man's head nodded. His chin hit his chest.

"Mr. Plinski!" A deep rumble came from Mr.

Plinski's chest. He wasn't dead. He was asleep.

The nurse came in and said, "I think he needs to rest now."

Nick couldn't believe it. He'd finally found the one person who knew all about the trunk, and that person wasn't talking.

That evening, Nick searched for "Mack Morris" on the Internet. He found dozens of matches, including a dentist in New Jersey who specialized in pain-free dentistry, a Mack Morris Blues Band, and someone on an auction web site who was selling his collection of sugar packets he'd picked up from diners across the country.

Then he noticed an entry at the bottom of the screen.

> Mack Morris, the Mysterious Shade
> From 1940 to 1965, the Shade
> protected the streets of Granite
> City. Appearing at night, this
> shadowy figure...

Nick clicked on the link. An old comic book appeared on the screen. It showed a city street from a low angle and a man in a trench coat standing in the rain, smoking a cigarette. At the top of the comic were the words "Mack Morris, the Mysterious..." Then came the title, in big block letters: "SHADE."

Nick leaned close to the screen and stared at the

hat on the man's head.

It was a fedora, with a crescent moon etched into the hatband.

# Chapter 15

As soon as Nick got to school on Monday morning, Tony ran up to him waving a newspaper clipping. "Did you see this? It was in yesterday's paper."

**Hot Time at Movie Theater**
The Elm City Fire Department responded to a call at the Harmony Cinema at 11:45 on Saturday when witnesses reported that a bright red flash had struck the building. "It was like a laser beam," said Mrs. Frieda McFurble.

Following the flash, the building grew warm enough to set off the sprinkler system, though no fire actually broke out. Authorities are continuing to investigate.

"11:45," Nick said. "That's just after we were there."

"Yeah. Weird, huh? Too bad we missed it."

Nick nodded, but his mouth was too dry to speak. He wasn't sorry they missed it. He remembered the crystal vibrating in his pocket, and he had an odd feeling that it was connected with the incident at the theater somehow.

"Good morning, class," Mrs. Smelding said. "If you'll take your seats, I have your geography quizzes from last week." She gave Nick a sugary smile as she handed him his paper. "Well done, Nicholas."

"Thanks," he said weakly.

"A final reminder," Mrs. Smelding said as she handed back the quizzes. "This Friday is the all-school talent show. Is there anyone else who wanted to sign up?"

The talent show was the kind of event that could make or break you popularity-wise. If you were a hit, everyone wanted to be your friend. But if you were bad, or did something weird like playing the bassoon, you could count on eating lunch alone for the rest of your life.

Nick wanted to be in the talent show. He wanted to do something so incredible that everyone would be amazed. Unfortunately, to be in a talent show you needed talent, which he didn't have.

On the other hand, he did have the trunk.

His hand shot up.

"Yes, Nicholas?"

"I want to be in the talent show."

Snickers erupted around the room. "That's wonderful, Nicholas. I'm glad to see you taking an interest in school activities. What do you plan to do?"

He hadn't thought that far ahead. He just figured

81

he could do something with the stuff from the trunk. "I'm not sure."

The snickers turned to laughs and Mrs. Smelding said, "Well, I'll write your name down and you can let me know later."

As soon as class was over, Nick grabbed his hat and ran out, hoping to catch Sarah Williams so he could invite her to the party. Now that Mr. Plinski had fixed the hat, he didn't have to worry about inviting the whole school.

Harley Davison and his gang were coming down the hall.

Nick ducked behind an open door as Harley barged past, shoving kids out of the way. He was headed for Justin Howard, a new kid who hadn't joined any group yet. Justin seemed like a good guy and Nick thought maybe they could be friends.

Harley put an arm around Justin's shoulder. "Hey, Justy-baby. You want to go to a party after the talent show on Friday? It's going to be great."

"Where?"

"The chess club is putting it on. But you have to be invited by a member of the club. And I just happen to know someone who wants to take you."

Nick wondered who he was talking about. Harley wasn't even *in* the chess club.

Justin looked doubtful too. "Who is it?"

"Oh, she's real cute. Come on, I'll introduce you."

They headed down the hall and Nick followed at a safe distance. This didn't look good.

Harley turned a corner and stopped. "There she is," he said, pointing to Priscilla Grimes, who was putting books into her locker. She heard the commotion and turned around.

Justin's face fell. "That's her?"

"Yeah," Harley said. "Foxy, huh?" He burst out laughing and the rest of his gang joined in. Justin pretended to gag and punched Harley on the shoulder.

They took off down the hall, laughing and making gorilla noises, past a red-faced Priscilla, whose eyes filled with tears.

Nick sighed. It was an initiation, and it looked as if Justin had passed. He was a member of Harley's group now.

Nick felt sorry for Priscilla, but there wasn't anything he could do about it. Besides, he had more important things to think about. He had to find Sarah Williams.

He didn't have to look far. He turned around and there was Sarah, right behind him, her lips pressed tightly together. She'd seen what Harley had done, and she wasn't happy.

"Boys are such jerks," she said, brushing past him.

"But—"

Sarah's friends shoved past him too. "Jerks," one of them said.

Nick stared as the girls paraded down the hallway. Thanks to Harley, he'd blown the perfect chance to ask Sarah to the party. He thought about running after Sarah. But there were too many people around. What if the hat acted up again? What if...

A voice came from behind him. "Having trouble with your locker?"

It was Mr. McCloskey.

"I said, did you need help with your locker?"

"No, thanks," Nick said. He retreated down the hallway, glancing back over his shoulder. Mr. McCloskey gave him that look again, the one that said, *I'm watching you.*

# Chapter 16

Nick ran to math class, where Mr. Dillard was handing out test sheets. "Put away your books," he said. "As well as your cheat sheets, cell phones, and secret decoder rings." This sounded like a joke, but you could never tell with Mr. Dillard, since he never seemed to crack a smile.

It didn't matter. Nick didn't need any cheat sheets. He had his magic glasses.

Mr. Dillard finished handing out the tests. "You may begin."

Nick spun the dial to the future setting. A large, red F sat at the top of his paper.

He gulped. It was a good thing he had the glasses. He read the first question.

1. If a train leaves Missoula, Montana traveling east at 60 miles per hour, how long will it take to get to Helena, which is 110 miles away?

Nick stared at the page. He'd been expecting multiple-choice questions. How were the glasses supposed to help him with this? He glanced at the rest of the page. The whole test was problems.

He took a guess and wrote "30 minutes." The grade was still F.

He erased his answer and tried "25 minutes."

F.

He tried 17 minutes, 35 minutes, and 1 1/2 hours. None of them worked. The F was superglued to the page.

He decided to skip that question. He went through the rest of the test, making guesses and looking at the top of the page each time. It was always F.

He stuck his hand in his pocket and fiddled with the pocket watch, clicking the stem. This was a disaster. What was he supposed to do?

The classroom fell quiet, the way it did whenever the principal walked in.

Nick looked up. No one moved, no one made a sound. Audrey O'Malley was bent over her paper, pencil poised above it, motionless. Tony stared up the ceiling as if he expected to see the answers there. In the back of the room, Eric Newman had a finger up his nose, but the finger wasn't moving. Even the aquarium, which had been bubbling noisily, was silent.

But the weirdest sight of all was Sarah Williams, whose hair seemed to be frozen in mid-air. It was as if time had stopped while she was flipping it away from her face.

As if time had stopped.

Nick yanked the watch from his pocket. The second hand had stopped at a little past 10:15. He stuck it back in his pocket and clicked the stem.

The aquarium started bubbling, Audrey's pencil scritched over the paper, and Sarah's hair finished its flip. Nick spun around to look at Eric, who turned red and stuffed his hands into his pockets.

Nick clicked the watch again. Pencils halted, the aquarium fell silent, the clock on the wall froze.

Another click and the classroom came back to life.

Nick slumped in his chair, gripping the watch. This was unbelievable—a watch that stopped time! Imagine what he could do with it!

*"Nick! Time to go to bed. And don't argue with me because you know it's way past—"*

Click.

*"Hello, this is the Peabody Library calling to remind you that the video game "Attack Quest" is overdue. If it is not returned today, we'll have to charge you a—"*

Click.

*"Man, can you believe it's the last day of summer already? It seems as if summer just started and now we have to go back—"*

Click.

*"Nick! Don't use up all the hot water in the shower! You've been in there for—"*

"Ten minutes."

Nick snapped awake as Mr. Dillard said, "You have ten minutes left."

Nick looked at his paper. Ten minutes? He had barely started. There was no way he could finish. He needed more…

Time.

A sly smile spread across his face. He didn't need more time. In fact, he had all the time in the world.

# Chapter 17

Nick clicked the watch. Instantly, Mr. Dillard was petrified. In fact, the entire class looked like a wax museum.

Now he had plenty of time for the test. He could just walk around the room and look at everyone else's papers. He could go to the library and look up the answers. In fact, he could go to Missoula, Montana and look up the answers. Who would know?

He walked around the room looking over the other kids' shoulders, but quickly realized he had a problem—everyone had different answers. How was he supposed to know who had the right answers? What he needed was an answer sheet.

Of course—Mr. Dillard always kept the answer sheets in his office.

Nick stuck his head into the hallway. At the end of the hall, a teacher stood frozen, tacking a notice to a bulletin board.

Good. Time was stopped everywhere, not just in Mr. Dillard's room.

He jogged to Mr. Dillard's office, turned the corner, and stopped.

There, standing in front of Mr. Dillard's desk, was Mr. McCloskey, his back to the door and a mop in his hands.

Great—Mr. McCloskey was right in the way. Nick thought for a moment and pulled out the watch. He'd just have to restart time and give Mr. McCloskey a chance to move.

He ducked behind the door, clicked the watch and counted to ten. Then he stopped time again.

Mr. McCloskey had moved in front of the filing cabinet. Nick squeezed by him and rummaged through Mr. Dillard's desk. There were gum wrappers, old letters and sports magazines, but no answer sheets.

The only other place to look was the filing cabinet. He wished he'd checked there before Mr. McCloskey moved.

He stepped outside the office, started time for ten seconds, then clicked the watch again.

When he looked back in the office, Mr. McCloskey had barely moved.

"Rats."

He started time again and counted to twenty this time. Mr. McCloskey still hadn't moved. It was almost as if he knew Nick needed to get in the filing cabinet and was purposely blocking him.

On top of the filing cabinet was a small mirror. Nick looked in it and could see out in the hallway, right where he'd been standing when he restarted time. Had Mr. McCloskey seen him out there?

It didn't matter. Mr. McCloskey wasn't going to move. Nick would just have to go back to the class and look at someone else's test.

When Nick got back to the room, Mr. Dillard was standing behind his desk, staring at Nick's empty seat, a frown on his face.

Nick gulped. Mr. Dillard must have looked up while he was looking for the answer sheet. To Mr. Dillard, it would look as if Nick had simply disappeared.

He slid into his seat, picked up his pencil as if he'd been working all along and clicked the watch.

Nothing happened.

He clicked it again.

Still nothing.

"Come on, come on," he said, clicking the watch again and again.

It was no use. The watch was stuck. And so was he.

*Nick Herriman stared into the crevice between the massive glaciers, his feet teetering on the edge. He had been traveling for ages, decades perhaps—he didn't really know how long it had been. He only knew he had traveled a long way, across the continent and up into Alaska, the largest state in the United States.*

*It seemed fitting, somehow, to end it all in this frozen place. He had been stuck for too long between two ticks of a clock. It was like being in prison, only worse. At least in prison, he might have had someone to talk to. At least he might have heard a human voice.*

*The wind blew across the crevice, and in the moaning sound he imagined he heard a voice calling to him. "Nick...Nick..."*

"Nick?"

He looked up. Mr. Dillard was staring at him with an odd expression. "Where...I mean what..." He shook his head as if to clear it. "Is everything all right?"

Nick pulled out the watch. The second hand was moving again. Time had restarted.

"Everything's fine," he said. In fact, everything was great. He was free! The world was running again!

"Well, time's up," Mr. Dillard said. "Hand in your paper."

He passed his paper forward, complete with the big red F on top. As he did, Mr. McCloskey walked by the door carrying his ladder. He looked in, saw Nick, and gave him The Look again.

# Chapter 18

At breakfast the next morning, Nick said to his mother, "Can I go to Tony's house after school?"

"I suppose so. But be careful coming home. It's getting dark earlier these days."

"Great," he said, grabbing his backpack and the fedora.

"And don't forget to wear your jacket. I don't want you to catching—"

"OK, OK. I'll be careful."

Somehow, Nick managed to avoid Harley that whole day. But as he and Tony got on the bus that afternoon, Harley walked up to him, grinning.

"Hey, Ridiculous. Did you hear the good news?"

Nick looked at him doubtfully. "What?"

"We're going to be riding together."

Harley stuck a piece of paper under his nose.

> Due to changes in scheduling, we will be combining some bus routes and eliminating others. Starting tomorrow morning, students who ride Bus 27 will be riding Bus 13 instead. The bus will pick up students from the Bus 13 route, then those from Bus 27.

Nick rode on Bus 27. Bus 13 was Harley's. By the time it got to Nick's corner, the only empty seats would be in the back. And no one sat in the back of Harley's bus unless they were copying homework, playing poker, or planning to commit murder.

Harley stuffed the paper in Nick's pocket. "See you in the morning, loser." He walked away, laughing demonically.

"Whoa," Tony said as they got on the bus. "Bad news for those of us who are targets of the Harlinator."

"You're telling me," Nick said.

"As your best friend, I should tell you that your GameStation III would probably go to waste if you left it to anyone else."

Nick glared at him.

"Just a thought," Tony said.

As they rode home, Nick stared out the window. What was he going to do? If he rode that bus tomorrow, he would be dead meat.

The bus stopped to drop off some kids and Nick gazed idly at a street sign on the corner: Paradise Lane.

*Paradise Lane.* Where had he seen that before?

Then it came to him. That was the street Mr. Plinski's son had written in the register at the nursing home.

That gave him an idea. But he had to act now. His new bus probably wouldn't come this way. It was now or never.

He stood up and joined the kids who were getting off.

"Hey," Tony said. "Where are you—"

"I'll explain later," he said. Much later.

He hoped the driver wouldn't notice that this wasn't his usual stop. He didn't. The door squealed shut behind him and the bus took off with a hiss of its brakes.

Nick stared down Paradise Lane. He wasn't sure this would work, but it was worth a try. Mr. Plinski might not have all his marbles, but maybe Mrs. Plinski did.

He walked down the street, trying to look as if he belonged there. The other kids dropped off one by one, heading into their houses.

He took his time, checking the mailboxes as he went. Most of the boxes had numbers on them, and a few had names as well. What if the Plinskis didn't have their name on theirs? He didn't want to go knocking on doors to find the right house.

And what if Mrs. Plinski wasn't home? Or worse, what if her son *was* home? He didn't seem like the kind of guy who would understand about a trunk full of clothes that gave you magic powers. He might even want it back. Maybe this hadn't been such a good idea after all.

At the end of Paradise Lane was a run-down ranch with pale yellow paint peeling off it and a patchy lawn with several varieties of weeds. The mailbox at the end of the driveway read, *#8 - Plinski*.

The driveway was empty, but as Nick walked to the front door he heard a television coming from inside.

He pressed the doorbell. A moment later, footsteps shuffled to the door.

Mrs. Plinski opened the door a crack. "Yes? What can I do for you?"

"My name is Nick," he said. "I'm a...friend of your husband's." That wasn't exactly a lie. Mr. Plinski thought he was a friend, even if he didn't know *which* friend.

"Really?" Mrs. Plinski said, her face lighting up. "Come in, come in. Take your hat off."

Nick slipped the hat off and followed her to the living room, where a television blared a cooking show. Mrs. Plinski pointed him towards a beat-up sofa and lowered herself into a chair facing the television.

"Have you seen Nate lately?" she asked.

"Nate?"

"My husband. Nathan Plinski."

"Oh, sure," Nick said. "I saw him the other day. He seemed confused."

"That's because they're not feeding him right. A man is supposed to be in his right mind with the food they feed him there?"

Nick didn't know how long Mrs. Plinski's son would be gone and decided to get right to the point. "Mrs. Plinski, do you remember an old trunk your

96

husband had at his shop?"

She thought for a moment. "A big old black thing? With brass corners?"

"That's right. Do you remember where it came from?"

"I think his family brought it with them when they came to America. That's an old trunk, that is. It came from Warsaw."

"Warsaw?"

Mrs. Plinski raised her eyebrows. "You don't know where Warsaw is? It's in Poland. Don't they teach geography in school anymore?"

Nick turned red. He had no idea where Poland was. Then it hit him. *Poland.* The paper from the trunk was probably written in Polish.

He pulled out the paper. "I found this in the trunk," he said, "Can you tell me what it says?"

Mrs. Plinski squinted at the paper. "No. Yiddish, I can read. Gibberish, no."

"Gibberish?"

"Nonsense. Jibber jabber. Oh, it probably means something. Like a code, maybe. Nate was a nut for secret codes. I think it was because of his customers. They were all concerned about their privacy, as if they had secrets they were hiding. They always came in the back door, never the front door. And tight-lipped? You could get more information from a turnip."

On the television, a woman held up a triangular dumpling with crimped edges. "A kreplach is made of dough stuffed with meat or cheese," she said. "The secret to making a great kreplach..."

Mrs. Plinski waved a hand at the television. "Pish. She wouldn't know a good kreplach if she tripped over it." She looked back at Nick. "Where was I?"

"You were talking about your husband's customers."

"Oh, yes." She pointed a knobby finger at him. "The thing you have to understand, young man, is that my Nate's shop was no ordinary tailor shop."

"It wasn't?"

"I should say not." She raised her eyebrows. "He had a very unusual clientele."

"A what?"

"Clientele. It means customers. What, they don't teach you English either? Anyway, his customers were an odd bunch. It all started the day a man came into the shop wearing a hat just like yours."

Nick held up the fedora. "This one?"

"That one. A very mysterious man, he was. Mister..." She looked up at the ceiling.

"Morris?"

"That's it. You know him? A nice man, but very private. Anyway, he comes in through the back door and he waits until no one else is around. Then he pulls Nate aside and shows him the hat. He's whispering, Nate's whispering, and finally Nate says, 'OK, I think I can do it.'"

The host of the cooking show rolled out dough on a board. "Now you have to roll the dough very, very thin..."

"Thin?" Mrs. Plinski said. "She should know thin. My dough was like a feather. Like a feather."

"What about the hat?" Nick asked.

"Oh yes, the hat. So the man comes back the next day, and Nate gives him the hat, spiffed up like new. The man is thrilled. He tells Nate he's going to send all his friends to Plinski's Tailor Shop."

She threw her hands up in the air. "Well, after that, you wouldn't believe the people who came into the shop. People wearing masks and capes, people dressed up like the American flag. Cowboys, people in animal skins, all kinds of outlandish get-ups. Oh, it was crazy. Pretty soon, that's all Nate was doing, making costumes for those people, doing repairs for them."

Nick leaned closer, his heart racing. "Who were they?"

"Who else would they be?" Mrs. Plinski said. "Actors, of course."

"Actors?"

"Theater people. At least, that's what I figured. Who else would dress up like that?"

Nick could only think of one other group of people who would dress like that.

"So where does the trunk come in?"

"The trunk? Oh, that. That's where Nate put things that he didn't know what else to do with. You know, when you have something that's broken and you're not sure how to fix it, but it's too good to throw away? So Nate threw it into the trunk. Or maybe a customer would forget an item and leave it behind. Into the trunk it went. It was like a junk box."

Of course, Nick thought. That explained why the things in the trunk didn't always work right.

The woman on the TV said, "Next, we'll be making potato latkes..."

"Hah," Mrs. Plinski said. "This I've got to hear." She aimed a remote at the screen and turned up the volume. "With a name like O'Brien she should know latkes from liverwurst."

Nick sighed. Keeping Mrs. Plinski on track was like steering a go-cart with a bad tire. He began to think he'd gotten all the information from her that he was going to. "I should go now," he said.

"All right," Mrs. Plinski said, her eyes glued to the television. "You can let yourself out. But come again some time."

Nick ran home, thinking about what Mrs. Plinski had said. She was probably right about the paper. It wasn't a foreign language, it was a secret code. But he didn't think Mr. Plinski's customers were actors. He had a good idea who they were, though. And he remembered what Mr. Plinski had said. *Other people have secrets too.*

Nick spent that evening trying to decipher the code on the paper, but he didn't have any luck. He stared at it until his eyes hurt.

"Btrsnldq," he read. What kind of word was that? Even if you mixed the letters up, you didn't get anything that made sense.

Eventually, he gave up and went to bed. He was still thinking about the paper as he drifted off to sleep.

*General Lee Speekin, head of the National Space Bureau, looked tired. He'd been at his computer for hours. "I'm sorry to bother you, Herriman, but you're the best codebreaker we've got."*

*Nick Herriman, Cryptographer First Class, studied the computer. "What's the problem?"*

*"As you know, we've been picking up signals from the Gibberish quadrant for a few days now. We've been trying to decrypt the signals, but we haven't gotten anywhere. Then, just a few hours ago, our remote sensors picked this up." An image appeared on the screen, an odd triangular shape that was crimped at the edges.*

*Nick leaned closer to the screen. "What is it?"*

*"It's either an extraterrestrial space vehicle or the world's largest flying kreplach. Given the signals it's sending out, we've ruled out the kreplach theory."*

*"Can you play the signals for me?"*

*The general punched another button. A voice rumbled from the speakers, low and ominous, like thunder in the distance. It was an alien voice, but it sounded oddly familiar. "Advzqd, eddakd dzqsgkhmfr!" the voice said. "H zl Ynazq, bnmptdqnq ne sgd fzkzwx. Xnt ltrs nadx ld!"*

# Chapter 19

The next morning, Nick yelled down the stairs. "Mom, where are my sneakers?"

"I put them in the wash. They were filthy from that baseball game the other night."

Nick fished his sneakers out of the washing machine. They were still soaking wet. Now what was he supposed to wear for gym?

Then he remembered the winged shoes in the trunk. They weren't exactly gym shoes and they were too big for him. But maybe they'd work if he laced them as tight as he could.

He pulled the shoes out of the trunk. They smelled like laundry soap—probably from the Great Cleaning Incident. But they did look better than they had. They would have to do.

As he stuffed the shoes into his backpack his mother yelled, "Nick, hurry up or you'll miss the bus."

The bus.

Today was the day he'd be riding Harley's bus. In all the excitement, he'd forgotten about that—not to mention his impending death at the hands of Harley.

What was he going to do? If he got on that the bus, Harley would turn him into Nickburgers.

Then he saw the purple shirt lying on top of the trunk.

That was it. If he wore the purple shirt, Bus 13 would be serving Chicken McHarley instead of Nickburgers.

He put the shirt on and rolled up the sleeves so the rip wouldn't show—he could ask his mother to sew it later—and headed down to breakfast.

His mother saw the shirt and raised her eyebrows. "Are you wearing that to school?"

"Sure. Why not?"

"Well..." She hesitated. "You realize it's a woman's blouse, don't you?"

"It is?"

"Sure. See the buttons? They're on a different side from men's shirts."

"Oh." Nick ran back upstairs, his ears burning. That was close. A guy could survive a lot of things, but wearing a woman's blouse to school wasn't one of them.

Now what? There was no way he was going to ride the Bus of Doom without some kind of protection. As he threw on a t-shirt he yelled downstairs, "Mom, can I ride my bike to school?"

"Nick, I've told you before. You can't ride your bike on the highway until you have a helmet."

That was always her answer. And she always managed to find a reason that they couldn't afford a helmet. "But Mom—"

"No, Nicholas. That road is just too busy. You could get hurt."

Maybe. But if he took Harley's bus he would

103

*definitely* get hurt.

Then he remembered the mind-reading helmet. True, it was dorky looking. But looking dorky was better than looking dead.

He grabbed the helmet and ran down to the kitchen. "Mom, I've got a helmet. It was in the trunk."

She looked it over doubtfully. "I don't know. It looks pretty old."

"Yeah, but it's solid, see?"

He put the helmet on and immediately heard his mother's voice. *That highway is so busy. He's just like his father. He's not careful enough. He'll get hurt—*

"Mom," Nick said, looking her in the eyes. "You can't protect me from everything. Just because Dad died in an accident doesn't mean I will. I'll be careful."

She stared at him, frowning. *How did he know what I was thinking?*

"All right," she said finally. "But don't ride too fast. Watch out for traffic. And I want you to stop at every intersection and look both ways before you cross."

"Great!" he said, racing for the door. "See you later."


Nick rode to school, planning his day. The fedora was in the hatbox in his backpack—he wasn't taking any chances on messing it up again.

As he pulled up to the bike stand he saw Tony and called to him. "Here," he said, and handed him a slip of paper. "See if you can figure this out."

"What is it?"

"A secret code." He had copied the letters "rsdl rshbjr" from the yellow paper—no way was he giving Tony the whole sheet, in case he did figure it out.

"OK," Tony said, stuffing the paper into his pocket.

Nick locked his bike to the rack and looked up to see Harley and his gang walking towards him.

"Hey, Ridiculous, where were you? We missed you on the bus."

Nick ignored him and headed for the front door. Harley and the goon squad followed behind.

"What's this?" Harley said, rapping on the helmet. "Does your grandmother know you have her football helmet?"

Nick stopped and stared at Harley, his heart pounding. He'd had just about enough. He was sick of being pushed around. He was sick of the stupid jokes and the name-calling. Besides, Harley was already going to kill him, so it didn't matter.

"At least my grandmother gives me presents," he said.

"Hey, my grandmother gives me presents," Harley said.

Nick stared at him for a moment. "I don't mean Spider-Man underwear."

Harley's jaw dropped. He looked as if he wanted

to say something, but no sound came out.

"Whoa, Spider-Man," Justin said. "I bet those are cool."

"He's crazy," Harley said. "That helmet must have cooked his brain."

Nick ran into school before his life expectancy decreased significantly.

Harley called after him. "Hey, Ridiculous. Coach told me we're running the cross country course in gym today. I hope you know how to run."

# Chapter 20

Gym class came sooner than Nick wanted. In the locker room, Coach Zeoli told everyone to meet him outside by the track.

Nick waited until the other guys had left the locker room, then pulled the winged shoes out of the backpack. For the first time, he noticed that they didn't have any laces. Why hadn't he noticed that before? How was he supposed to tighten them up?

He put the shoes on anyway, hoping he'd be able to figure it out. Just as he had suspected, they were way too big for him.

Coach Zeoli appeared in the locker room door. "C'mon, Herriman! Everyone's waiting."

"Coach, I don't have—"

He felt something on his feet and looked down. The shoes had shrunk, molding themselves to fit his feet perfectly.

"You don't have what?" Coach asked.

"Nothing," Nick said.

"Then, come on. Move it!"

He followed Coach out to the track behind the school. The cross country course ran around the track, through the park next to the school, then back again. When the whole class had gathered at the starting line, Coach held up his stopwatch and yelled, "Go!"

They took off. Nick tried to stay in the middle of the pack, which seemed like the safest place to be.

Tony pulled ahead of him and yelled, "Come on, slowpoke."

"I'll catch up with you," Nick said. "I'm pacing myself."

He looked back. Harley and his gang, who normally led the runners, had held back too. By the time Nick got to the edge of the school property, it was just him and Harley's gang bringing up the rear. And they were closing in.

As everyone else ran into the park, Nick turned and headed back toward the school.

"Get him!" Harley yelled.

Nick ran as fast as he could, but it wasn't fast enough. They were gaining on him.

"Come on," Nick said to himself. *"Run!"*

He wasn't sure what happened next. In an instant, the rest of the world slowed down. He felt as if he were on one of those moving sidewalks at the airport, where you pass people who look as if they're walking in slow motion.

Nick looked back. Harley and the others seemed to be running in molasses. A bird flew by, moving so slowly that Nick could see its wings flapping. Leaves drifted from the maple tree in front of the school as if they were falling through syrup.

Nick looked down. It was the shoes. They hadn't done anything until he said "run," as if they were voice activated. There was only one way to find out.

"Faster!"

Instantly, Nick was kicked into high gear. He passed the front of the school as a mailman came out the front door. The mailman looked around, wondering where the sudden breeze had come from.

In a split-second, Nick ran the entire length of the school. He turned the corner and headed back to the track. At this rate, he could catch up with the others and finish the course with them. In fact, he could probably beat them. With these shoes, he would beat anybody.

*"We're here at the finals of the Olympic Cross Country event, and it looks as if Nick Herriman, the startling new runner from the United States, is going to take the gold medal. He has swept past the rest of the field, and he doesn't even look tired, ladies and gentlemen! There's just one more turn in the race and...Wait! What's this? Nick Herriman has taken a wrong turn. He's headed off course!"*

Nick snapped out of his daydream as he turned a corner. In front of him was a brick wall, and he was headed for it at full speed.

"Stop!"

The shoes stopped. Unfortunately, Nick didn't. At least, not right away. He landed flat on his face, missing the brick wall by two inches.

He heard Harley's voice in the distance behind him. "He must have gone around here. We've got him now!"

Nick was trapped. There was a door in the wall, but he had no idea where it went.

"Please don't be locked," Nick said and pushed on the handle.

The door opened into a hallway by the maintenance office. Nick ran in, slammed the door and leaned against it. Breathing hard, he pressed an ear to the door, listening for Harley.

"What do you think you're doing?" said a voice.

Nick spun around. It was Mr. McCloskey.

# Chapter 21

Mr. McCloskey stared at Nick. "I said, what are you doing?"

"Nothing."

"You know you're not supposed to be in here now."

"I know, but I was being chased by..." He decided not to get specific, for health reasons. "...by some kids. And I was trying to get away, and I—"

Mr. McCloskey stared at him. "Where did you get those glasses?"

"I found them."

He pointed to the winged shoes. "And those?"

"Uh...a friend gave them to me."

Mr. McCloskey nodded toward the maintenance office. "Come with me."

They went into the office and Mr. McCloskey closed the door. He pulled up a chair for Nick and sat in an old wooden swivel chair behind his desk. "Now tell me where you got those things."

Nick said nothing.

"You've got a choice," Mr. McCloskey said. "You can either tell me what's going on, or we'll go to the principal's office."

Nick shrugged. He didn't care.

"And he'll probably call your mother."

"What?" That would be a disaster. His mother

would get all upset about Harley, and she'd probably ask questions about the glasses, the shoes, and the other stuff in the trunk. "I didn't steal them," he said. "Honest."

Mr. McCloskey looked at him for a while. "No, I don't think you did."

That was a relief. So why did he care about them?

"You know," Mr. McCloskey said. "I've been watching you. I knew something was up with you. But I wasn't sure about it until I saw those shoes." He pointed to them. "Can I see them?"

"I guess so." Nick took the shoes off and handed them over.

As he examined the shoes, Mr. McCloskey sniffed them and said, "Did someone wash these?"

"My mother," Nick said.

McCloskey shook his head. "You're lucky you didn't get yourself killed with them."

"I am?"

"These were an early version. You're not supposed to put them in water. It messes up the positronic speed control."

Nick's mouth fell open. "How do you know that?"

Mr. McCloskey was silent for a moment, then turned to a bookshelf behind him. He pulled out a large book and set it on the desk.

He began flipping through it. It was a scrapbook, filled with photographs and newspaper clippings. He came to a page, stopped and pointed to a newspaper clipping. "See that?"

The headline read:

Kid Comet Nails Bank Robbers

Below it was a grainy photograph of a teenager in a superhero costume holding two crooks by their collars.

He was wearing the winged shoes.

Nick stared at the photograph. "These are his shoes?"

"They were his shoes."

Beneath the headline were the words, "Hal McCloskey, *Post Tribune* reporter."

"Is that you?" Nick asked.

Mr. McCloskey nodded. "I was a newspaper reporter for twenty years. Go on, turn the page."

Nick scanned the next page, then the one after that, flipping through the rest of scrapbook. All the stories were about superheroes, crime fighters and private eyes. Every one of the stories was written by Hal McCloskey.

"Are these real people?" Nick asked.

"Sure they are."

"But I didn't think—"

"You didn't think superheroes were real? They are where I come from."

Nick didn't recognize the names of any of the newspapers. Wherever Mr. McCloskey came from, it wasn't near Peabody. "And you knew them all?"

"Most of them. In fact, I know a lot more than you can imagine." He lowered his eyebrows. "Now maybe you should tell me exactly where you got those shoes."

Nick looked around, stalling for time. If he told anyone about the trunk, they wouldn't believe him. And if they *did* believe him, they'd probably take it away from him.

On the other hand, Mr. McCloskey already knew about the shoes. And maybe he could help Nick figure out the rest of the stuff in the trunk. In fact, Mr. McCloskey was probably the perfect person to talk to. He was quiet and kept to himself. He wasn't likely to run around telling everyone Nick's secrets. Given how slowly Mr. McCloskey moved, it was hard to imagine him running anywhere.

Nick took a deep breath. "It all started at the swap shop."

"The swap shop?"

Nick told him about the trunk. He told him about the fedora, the glasses, and the helmet. He told him about flying around Peabody, almost getting swallowed by Max, stopping time, and dumping pudding on half the kids at Peabody School.

"Sounds as if you've had a bit of trouble," Mr. McCloskey said.

"A bit? I've had the extra-large, family-style, supersize, jumbo supply of trouble."

"Do your folks know about the trunk?"

"Are you kidding? If my mother knew, she'd have

114

a fit. She worries about me *crossing* the street, let alone flying over it."

"What about your father?"

Nick hesitated. "He's not around."

"So he's not going to be much help with this."

"It's not his fault," Nick said. "He died when I was little." Nick didn't like talking about his father, and he only did it to make Mr. McCloskey drop the subject.

"What happened to him?"

"I don't know. It was a hit-and-run driver."

"I'm sorry," Mr. McCloskey said. "And I know it's not his fault. But he's still not around to help you at times like this, is he?"

That was true. There were times when a guy needed his dad to talk to, and this was definitely one of those times. "I just wish I knew where the stuff in the trunk came from," Nick said.

"Oh, that," Mr. McCloskey said. "I can tell you that."

Nick stared at him. "You can?"

# Chapter 22

"You know that green helmet?" Mr. McCloskey said. "That belonged to Mentalo, Reader of Minds. It got dented in a battle with Dr. Diablo and never worked right after that."

That explained the occasional gibberish, Nick thought.

"The flying rope was probably Captain Wonder's. He got his ropes from the Mystic Monks of Mahasa, in Tibet. The monks did good work, but the ropes tended to wear out after a while and develop problems."

"I'll say."

"The jeweled belt belonged to ExpandoMan," Mr. McCloskey said. "And it caused him no end of embarrassment. Imagine defeating an evil genius like Baron Malefico and then having your belt get stuck just as the reporters arrive."

"What about the bouncing boots?"

Mr. McCloskey shook his head. "You've got me there. Never heard of those before."

"But how do you know about all that other stuff?"

"When you're a reporter for twenty years, you learn things. And you learn to keep secrets."

"Now you sound like Mr. Plinski."

A slow smile spread across Mr. McCloskey's face. "Ah, Nathan Plinski."

"You know him?"

"I sure do. He was a good tailor—all the superheroes came to his shop—and he knew how to keep a secret too."

"You're telling me," Nick said. He explained about trying to get Mr. Plinski to reveal the secrets of the trunk. "His lips are closed tighter than a stuck gym locker."

"I'm not surprised," Mr. McCloskey said. "I'm betting the trunk was where he kept costumes he was working on, along with odds and ends that people left behind."

"That's what Mrs. Plinski said. But why would people leave stuff like that behind?"

Mr. McCloskey shrugged. "Just because you've got super-powers doesn't mean you remember where you left your car keys."

Nick had never thought of it that way. He always assumed that when you were a superhero you did everything right.

"So now that you've got this trunk, what are you going to do with it?" Mr. McCloskey asked.

"What do you mean?"

Mr. McCloskey stood, leaned against the side of the desk and crossed his arms, thinking. "Let me show you something else."

He pulled a key from the desk drawer and used it to unlock a tall gray cabinet in the corner. The door creaked open as if it hadn't seen daylight in a long time. Hanging inside were two uniforms, a large one and a slightly smaller one. In the bottom of the cabinet were two pairs of winged shoes just like Nick's.

Mr. McCloskey pulled out the larger uniform. It was green, with a bright yellow circle on the chest. Inside the circle was a pair of wings.

"Where did that come from?" Nick asked.

Mr. McCloskey reached into the top shelf of the cabinet, pulled out a comic book and handed it to Nick. "Take a look."

The comic showed a man in a costume just like the one Mr. McCloskey was holding. Across the top of the comic were the words "The Meteor," with little lines trailing after each letter.

"This belonged to the Meteor, the fastest man on the planet," Mr. McCloskey said. "The other one belonged to Kid Comet, his sidekick. The Meteor gave them to me as souvenirs when he retired."

"Retired?" Nick said. It hadn't occurred to him that superheroes would retire.

Mr. McCloskey shrugged. "You can't be a superhero forever. There comes a day when you have to hang up the uniform."

He hung the costume back in the cabinet. "This may surprise you, but there's not a lot of money in being a superhero. No one pays you for running faster than the wind, unless you do commercials. And then they want you to wear *their* shoes."

He stuck the comic book back on the shelf. "And most superheroes don't make a living at it. Take the

Fireman. His wife supported him for years, till he quit the business and opened a barbecue place."

"Barbecue?"

"That's right. Lou's Rib House, used to be out on Highway 28. Best flamed-broiled ribs in the East, and no one ever noticed that Lou had hardly any electric bill."

"What about Kid Comet?" Nick asked. "What happened to him?"

Mr. McCloskey got quiet again. "Let's just say he's not around anymore."

Nick wasn't sure what that meant, but it didn't sound good.

Mr. McCloskey closed the scrapbook and put it back on the shelf. "Here's what I'm saying. It's fine to have super powers, defeat evildoers and save the world now and then. But it's also nice to raise a family, help your neighbors and be a good citizen. There are all kinds of heroes in the world, you know."

Nick rolled his eyes. This was beginning to sound like civics class.

"You need to think about how you're going to use those things in the trunk," Mr. McCloskey said.

"That's the problem," Nick said. "I don't *know* how to use them."

"That's not what I meant. I meant, are you going to use the trunk selfishly? You know, to make yourself the smartest, strongest, most popular kid at Peabody School?"

Nick's ears turned red. "I don't know."

"Because you could use it to help other people."

"Like who?" Peabody School wasn't exactly crawling with evil geniuses and mutant monsters.

"Look around," Mr. McCloskey said. "There are people in need all over the place. But you have to decide. Are you going to use your powers for yourself, or for others?"

Nick didn't need a mind-reading helmet to know what Mr. McCloskey thought he should do. But that was easy for him to say. He wasn't likely to be voted the Average Kid of the Month, Year and Decade at Peabody School. And he wasn't about to be killed by Harley Davison.

The bell rang. "Think about it," Mr. McCloskey said. "In the meantime, be careful with that trunk. Some of those things could be dangerous if you don't use them correctly."

Mr. McCloskey was beginning to sound like Nick's mother. "OK," he said.

"And if you ever need help, call me." He wrote his phone number on a piece of paper and handed it to Nick.

Nick wasn't sure why he was being so helpful, but he took the paper and stuffed it into his pocket. He didn't think he'd ever use it, but you never knew.

By the time Nick made it to math class, he was late.

"Nice of you to join us, Mr. Herriman," Mr.

Dillard said as Nick fell into his seat.

Tony leaned over and said, "Hey, Flash. We missed you out there. Where did you disappear to?"

Nick shrugged. "Got a stitch in my side. Had to take it easy."

"I have an announcement," Mr. Dillard said, reading from a notice. "Today is the last day to sign up for the talent show tomorrow. Please see Mrs. Smelding if you are interested."

Tony leaned over to Nick. "You still planning on being in the show?"

"I don't know. I haven't come up with an act yet."

"Well, you could do your disappearing act, like in gym."

Nick started to think of a wise comeback, then stopped. "You know, that's a great idea."

# Chapter 23

After math class, Nick stopped by Mrs. Smelding's room and told her what he had in mind for the talent show.

"That sounds...interesting, Nicholas. I'm sure the other students will enjoy that."

He headed for his locker to get the fedora. Today was the last chance he'd have to ask Sarah to the party.

As he opened his locker, he felt a hand on his shoulder. He recognized the meaty hand even before he turned around. Harley. Fortunately, there were lots of other kids around. Safety in numbers.

"You were lucky in gym today," Harley said, poking a finger into Nick's chest. "But tomorrow's another day."

Great, Nick thought as Harley strutted off. Something to look forward to.

Harley passed Priscilla Grimes and mumbled, "Ook-ook." The rest of his gang picked up the call. "Ook-ook. Ook-ook-ook."

The hallway echoed with gorilla noises. Everyone looked at Priscilla—they knew who this was about.

Eventually, they all drifted away. But Priscilla stood in front of her locker, sniffling. In the back of Nick's mind, he heard Mr. McCloskey's voice. *There are people in need all over the place.*

All right, he'd give it a try.

He put the fedora on and waited until the hallway was completely empty except for him and Priscilla.

"Hey, Priscilla," he said quietly.

She closed her locker and stared at the door. "What?"

He pulled the hat down till it shaded his eyes. "Look at me."

She turned, her eyes brimming. He had never really noticed her eyes before, but now he saw that they were the same blue eyes he'd seen on the grown-up Priscilla in the cafeteria that day.

"What?" she asked.

"You are a nice person," Nick said.

Priscilla's face relaxed. A peaceful calm seemed to flow over her. "I am a nice person."

"You're smart, too."

"I'm smart, too." She seemed to be staring right through him.

Nick glanced up and down the hall. He had to finish this before anyone else saw him. "Forget about what just happened. In fact, from now on, ignore everything Harley says. He's a loser, but you're going to turn out just fine."

"Forget about what just happened. From now on—"

"Yeah, yeah, that's right. Just remember, you're going to turn out fine."

He started to leave, then turned back. "And if anyone asks, this was your own idea, OK?"

"This was my own idea," Priscilla mumbled.

"Right."

Nick went to his locker. He glanced back at Priscilla, who blinked as if she was just waking up. A grin spread over his face. Someday, she would thank him for this...

*At the podium, a man in a tuxedo tore open an envelope and pulled out a slip of paper. "And the Oscar for Best Actress goes to Priscilla Grimes for The Babe and the Bandit!"*

*The audience cheered as "Princess Priscilla"—the name the fan magazines had given her—strolled to the stage in her sequined gown.*

*"Well, Priscilla," the presenter said, handing the Oscar to her. "This has been quite a year for you, having only recently turned to film after a successful career as a supermodel. What do you have to say?"*

*A hush fell over the crowd. "I'd like to thank all the usual people—they know who they are. But I'd especially like to thank the man who made it all possible, the man who changed my life by making me believe in myself."*

*Priscilla flashed her million-dollar smile as a spotlight swept the audience and fell on a man in a gray fedora—Dr. Nicholas Herriman, best-selling author of Average No More."*

*"This is for you," Priscilla said. "The one. The only. Nicholas."*

"Nicholas?"

He blinked. "Huh?"

It was Audrey O'Malley and her friends. She

124

nudged one of them and snickered. "Isn't love wonderful?"

"No," Nick said quickly. "I was just..."

It was too late. They'd seen him staring at Priscilla again.

They took off and one of them whispered, "I wonder what their kids will look like?" The others burst into giggles.

Nick slammed his locker. So much for being a nice guy and helping others. If he knew Audrey, she'd post the news about him and Priscilla on her blog, nosystuckupblabbermouth.com, within the hour.

As he rode home that afternoon, Nick argued with himself about this hero business. He had tried helping someone else, and look what happened. From now on, he was going to worry about himself first. And his top priority was to keep from being killed by Harley.

The only way to do that was to decipher that list. But the only one who knew the code was Mr. Plinski, and he still wasn't talking.

He heard a squeak and looked down at his brakes. They seemed fine, but the sound grew louder. Then he realized the noise was coming from inside the helmet. He looked up.

A robin passed overhead. The squeak became a high-pitched voice. "*Looking for worms,*" it said. "*Looking for worms...looking for worms.*"

He screeched to a stop, laying rubber on the sidewalk.

Of course. That was it.

# Chapter 24

At the nursing home, Nick found Mr. Plinski nodding over a glass of milk and a plate of graham crackers. He looked up as Nick walked in. "Oh, it's you."

"How are you doing?" Nick said. "I brought something to show you."

"You did? What's that?"

Nick pulled out the yellow paper. Mr. Plinski glanced at it and said, "Again with the paper. I told you, I never saw that before."

Nick took the helmet out of his backpack. It was time to get serious.

Mr. Plinski eyed the helmet suspiciously. "And why are you showing me this?"

"Does it look familiar?"

"Maybe it does and maybe it doesn't. Who wants to know?"

"I do. I found it in the trunk."

"Ah," Mr. Plinski said. "I get it. Another test. Well, not to worry. I'll never tell."

Nick put the helmet on and Mr. Plinski said, "You think I don't know what you're doing? Well, it won't work." He closed his eyes, crossed his arms over his chest and hummed.

"What is the secret code?" Nick said.

Mr. Plinski kept humming. Inside the helmet Nick

heard him singing, *Mares eat oats, and does eat oats, and little lambs eat ivy...*

Nick slapped the side of the helmet. What a time for it to go on the fritz.

Mr. Plinski's voice sang, A kid'll eat ivy, too. Wouldn't you?

Nick sighed and took the helmet off. With all that nonsense, there was no way of telling what Mr. Plinski had really been thinking.

A grin creased Mr. Plinski's wrinkled face. "Nothing, right? What did I tell you?" He slapped Nick on the knee. "Stop worrying, my friend. I told you, Nathan Plinski knows how to keep a secret."

Nick stood to leave. He had to get home before his mother started to worry and called in the FBI to look for him. "See you later."

As he headed for the door, Mr. Plinski said, "It's funny. I had that old trunk for thirty years and no one cared about it. All of a sudden, everyone's interested in it."

Nick stopped. "What do you mean?"

"First you come in, then that nudnik with the mustache starts asking all kinds of questions."

"Your son?"

Mr. Plinski shrugged his thin shoulders. "I don't know who he is. He just came in asking about the trunk. Wanted to know who you were. But don't worry, I didn't tell him anything."

Nick raced home. As he ran in the back door, his

mother said, "Nick—"

"Hang on," Nick yelled. He ran up to his bedroom, opened the door and stopped in his tracks.

The trunk was gone.

He ran downstairs. "Mom, where's the trunk?"

"That's what I was trying to tell you. The man who owned it came by."

"A guy with a mustache?"

"That's right. Mr. Platski?"

"Plinski! And you let him take it?"

"Nick, that trunk belonged to his father. He said he'd been having second thoughts ever since he took it to the dump. I thought you'd understand. Imagine how you'd feel if your dad had a trunk and left it to you."

"Mom—"

"You know, you could stand to be more like your father. He was always thinking of other people, never about himself."

"I've got to go," Nick said, racing out the door.

"Where?"

"I have to go do something."

"Be careful!" she hollered after him.


In the little house on Paradise Lane, Mrs. Plinski was not happy with her son. "I still don't see why you wanted that smelly old trunk back."

Joseph Plinski had pulled everything out of the trunk, scattering shirts, shoes and accessories around the living room. "I told you, Ma, I'm looking for something."

"Like what?"

He ignored her, because he didn't know what he was looking for. He just knew the trunk was valuable. Why else would that nosy kid come snooping around, asking questions about it?

Joseph hadn't thought much about the kid visiting his father in the nursing home. As usual, his old man was tight-lipped about what the kid wanted. His father had never really trusted Joseph with the details of his business anyway. But Joseph's mother had spilled the beans about how the kid came snooping around, asking questions. Since the kid had left his address in the visitor's register at the nursing home, Joseph decided to pay him a visit—during school hours, of course, when he wasn't likely to be around and couldn't whine to his mother about Joseph taking the trunk.

"I'm sorry I even told you about the trunk," Mrs. Plinski said, pacing the living room. "He was such a nice boy. What do you want that old thing for anyway?"

"I told you..." Joseph heaved a sigh as he emptied the contents of the side compartments. "Never mind."

It hadn't been easy getting the trunk home—he'd almost had a heart attack lugging it into the house. But there had to be something special about the trunk—old stock certificates maybe, or real estate deeds—and he was determined to find out what it was.

So far, he'd found nothing but junk. Maybe the kid had taken the valuables out. But then, why would he come around asking all those questions about it?

Joseph reached into the last empty compartment and his hand hit a button on the side. He pressed it and the bottom of the compartment popped up.

"Aha!" He reached in and pulled out a gold medallion with engraving on it. He squinted at the medallion and read the words on it. "Gnosis, aoratos, metamorfosi, anoixis. Well, I'll be a monkey's uncle. This must be it!"

"What?" his mother asked.

He held the medallion up for her to see. That's when he noticed the coarse dark hairs sprouting out of the back of his hand.

# Chapter 25

Nick pedaled to the Plinski's house as fast as he could. He wasn't sure what he was going to say, but he had to get the trunk back.

He pulled up outside the house. From inside came the sound of screaming and glass breaking.

Nick knocked, but no one answered. He opened the door slowly. "Hello?"

"Help!" Mrs. Plinski yelled from the living room. "In here! Help!"

He ran to the living room. It was a wreck. The trunk sat in the middle of the floor, its contents scattered around. Hiding behind it, surrounded by broken glassware, was a terrified chimpanzee.

Mrs. Plinski stood in a corner holding a vase. "Get him away from me," she yelled. "I want my son back!"

The chimp was wearing a shirt that was way too big for him—the pants had already fallen off—and he was holding the owl medallion from the trunk.

"What happened?" Nick asked.

"My son..." Mrs. Plinski said. "That thing..." and then she screamed again.

"Eek-eek-eek-eek," the chimp said, holding up the medallion as if he were trying to explain.

Nick looked at him. "Mr. Plinski?"

The chimp nodded his head fiercely, "Eek-eek-

eek!"

"OK, calm down," Nick said. "Maybe I can help you."

The chimp whimpered and Nick said, "Let's leave your mother alone for a while." He took the chimp by the hand and led him into the next room.

"Eek-eek-eek," the chimp said, holding up the medallion again.

"I know," Nick said. "Maybe I should hold that for you." He grabbed the medallion and slammed the door shut before the chimp could argue with him.

The Plinski-chimp screeched in rage, pounding on the door.

Nick stuffed the medallion into his pocket and pulled out Mr. McCloskey's phone number. If he ever needed Mr. McCloskey's help, now was the time.

"Mrs. Plinski, can I use your phone?"

"Yes, yes. Just get that monkey out of here and bring back my Joey."

Mr. McCloskey's phone rang six times. "Come on, come on," Nick said, wishing Mr. McCloskey wasn't so darn slow.

"Hello?" Mr. McCloskey said at last.

"It's Nick. Nick Herriman. I've got a real problem here."

He explained the situation and Mr. McCloskey chuckled. "Serves him right. He's lucky he didn't turn himself into a pig."

"What should I do?"

"Nothing. He'll be back to normal in an hour or so. But he's going to have one heck of a headache when he comes around."

Mrs. Plinski tapped Nick on the arm. "What is he saying? What about Joey?"

"He's going to be fine," Nick said. "In a while."

"Good." She pointed to the trunk. "Now please, get that thing out of here. Trouble like that, I don't need."

Mr. McCloskey arrived a few minutes later and helped Nick carry the trunk to his van.

Hidden in the shadow of the trees behind the house stood a figure in a dark coat, watching them. The figure pointed a long finger at the van and muttered, "Clouds of darkness, descend." On the hand was a red ring with a lightning insignia on it.

Mr. McCloskey looked up at the sky as he and Nick got into the van. "That's funny. It's getting foggy all of a sudden."

It was more than foggy. As Mr. McCloskey started the van, a thick haze surrounded it. He turned on the lights as they rolled down the driveway, but that didn't help. It was as if they were inside a dark cloud.

"Can you see where you're going?" Nick asked.

"No. I'm going to have to pull over."

He steered the van to the side as they came to the end of the Plinski's driveway. At that moment, they drove out of the fog.

They looked back at the Plinski's house. It was

covered in thick fog, like a giant, igloo-shaped cloud surrounding it.

"That's strange," Nick said.

"Extremely odd," Mr. McCloskey said.

Of course, it was nothing compared to what had happened to Mr. Plinski's son. Nick nodded towards the Plinski's house. "What happened back there?"

"That's what happens when people fiddle with things they don't understand."

"You mean this?" Nick said, holding up the medallion.

"Yes. That medallion once belonged to a hero named the Enchanter. It provided him with a number of powers—invisibility, supernatural wisdom, the ability to turn into different kinds of animals. But the effects only last for an hour."

Nick turned the medallion over in his hand. "How does it work?"

"I'm not sure. I suspect it involves the inscription."

Nick studied the words again. "Gnos—"

"Don't," Mr. McCloskey said, clamping his hand over the medallion. "You've already seen what it can do to someone who doesn't know how to use it."

Nick shivered, picturing himself turned into a porcupine or a slug. "What happened to the Enchanter?"

Mr. McCloskey shook his head. "He was in a battle with a villain named Nocturno, the Lord of Darkness. The Enchanter disappeared, and nobody ever found out what happened to him."

Nick rested his head against the back of the seat, thinking. "What happened to the rest of the superheroes?"

Mr. McCloskey gave him a glance, then looked back at the road. "It's a long story. Maybe I'll tell you about it someday."

Back at Nick's house, Mr. McCloskey helped him carry the trunk in. They agreed not to tell Nick's mother about the incident, only that Mr. Plinski decided he didn't want the trunk back after all.

After Mr. McCloskey left, Nick pulled everything out of the trunk and sorted through it. They'd been in such a hurry to leave the Plinskis' that they'd just tossed everything in.

At the bottom of the trunk he found the blue crystal. But it was cracked, and the dark blue center glowed through the crevice, as if something inside wanted to get out.

Nick stuck a fingernail into the crack and pried it open. The crystal broke into a half-dozen pieces. In the middle of the fragments lay a blue ring. It looked as if it had been cut from a single piece of brilliant gemstone, and there was a lightning bolt inscribed on the top.

The ring glowed, as if it was happy to be released from the crystal. Then it vibrated for a second, just like the crystal had outside the movie theater.

Nick tried it on. It was too big, but if he clenched

his fist, it stayed on.

He pointed the ring at his bureau, lowered his voice and said, "Up! Rise! Ascend!"

The bureau ignored him.

He imagined a giant blue hand coming out of the ring and picking it up.

Nothing happened.

It was hard to believe this was just an ordinary ring, given everything else that had happened. At least it looked expensive—it would go well with the costume he had in mind for the talent show. He dug some string out of his desk drawer and looped it through the ring several times until it was snug enough to stay on.

The phone rang and his mother yelled, "Nick, it's for you."

It was Tony. "I figured out that code," he said.

"You did? What does it say?"

"Stem sticks."

"Stem sticks?"

"Right. So what does it mean?"

Nick had no idea. What were stem sticks? Flowers had stems…

And so did watches.

He pulled out the pocket watch and stared at it. "The stem sticks," he said.

"What?" Tony asked.

"Never mind," Nick said. Now he knew for sure the list was about the things in the trunk. "How did you figure it out?"

"Ah, zat vas no problem for a zuperior intellect like mine."

"Right, right. But how did you do it?"

"Hey, if you're going to invent a secret code, you have to make it more complicated than that."

"No, I mean, exactly what did you do to decipher it?"

"I told you, it was easy. I just added..." Tony stopped. "Wait a minute. If you invented the code, don't you know how it works?"

"Sure, but—"

"You don't know, do you?"

"Of course I do. I just—"

"So who wrote it?"

"Never mind," Nick said. "Got to go. I'll talk to you later."

He hung up, ran to his junk drawer and dug around till he found a small bottle of lubricating oil. He squirted two drops of oil on the watch stem and clicked it a few times. As he did, the clock on his nightstand stopped, then started, stopped and started again.

Max walked into his room...then stopped...started...stopped again.

"Like clockwork," Nick said. "Get it, Max? Like clockwork?"

Max whined and collapsed at his feet.

Everyone was a critic. But he didn't care. Now he had everything he needed for the best talent act in history.

After this, he'd have so many friends he wouldn't have to worry about Harley. By this time tomorrow he would be Nick Herriman, Superstar.

**Peabody Police Report**
Domestic complaint.
Police responded to a Paradise Lane residence, where a woman complained that her son had made a monkey of himself. Officers suggested that the woman and her son seek family therapy to help resolve their issues.

# Chapter 26

Nick woke the next morning to the sound of his mother yelling, "Oh, no. I can't believe it."

He stumbled downstairs, still half asleep. His mother stood with the back door open. Outside, covering the door, were thick strands of sticky white stuff, like a giant spider's web.

Nick looked out the windows. They were covered with the stuff too. In fact, the whole house seemed to be covered in it.

"Darned kids," his mother said. "And it's not even Halloween."

"Yeah," Nick said weakly. But he knew this wasn't just any kids. It had to be Harley. On the other hand, this seemed extreme, even for Harley. Besides, how could he pull off a stunt like that like that without them noticing?

Nick got dressed for school while his mother grabbed a yardstick and cleared the stuff away from the door. "Come on, I'll drive you to school," she said.

As they drove off, a figure stood across the street, in the shadows by their neighbor's garage. "You will not escape me forever," the figure murmured.

Nick had planned out his day to avoid running into Harley. He just had to make it through the day and get to the talent show without being killed. After that, he'd be OK—better than OK.

After the final period, the entire school gathered in the auditorium for the show. Nick stood backstage with the rest of the performers. He was dressed in his suit and vest, with the fedora on his head, the blue ring on his hand, and the gold rope wrapped around his waist. The pocket watch hung by its gold chain from his belt.

Mrs. Smelding said, "Nicholas, come with me. I want to make sure everyone is lined up before we begin. You'll be our last performer."

That was fine with him. When he was done, no one would remember the other acts anyway.

Principal Watkins emceed the talent show, which was a mix of the good, the bad, and the incredibly lame. Tony and Owen did the "Who's on First" routine and got lost half way through it. Two girls sang a sappy song about being best friends forever. A band called Definite Blue played a loud version of an old Beatles song—or maybe a Nike commercial; it was hard to tell. Other kids danced and twirled batons and played saxophones that sounded like wounded elephants.

The next to last performer was Priscilla Grimes, who was going to sing. No contest, as far as Nick was concerned.

Then Priscilla began to sing, and he realized it might be a contest after all. She was singing some song about having wind under your wings, and she was really good. Who would have guessed that?

He noticed she had done something different with her hair. And for once, she wasn't wearing her glasses—had she gotten contacts? She looked—well, almost cute. Maybe that talk he'd had with her was starting to do some good.

As Priscilla sang, a sound came from the middle of the auditorium—just loud enough to hear but not so loud that you could tell where it was coming from: "Ook-ook."

Nick peeked out past the curtains. In the center of the seats, slumped down in his seat, was Harley Davison, making gorilla noises.

Harley's friends on either side of him picked up the chant.

"Ook-ook. Ook-ook-ook."

The teachers looked around but couldn't pinpoint the culprits, and they didn't want to interrupt Priscilla's performance to find out who it was.

Priscilla heard though, and her eyes filled with tears. She faltered and missed a line. She stumbled through the rest of the song, forgetting some words, hitting wrong notes, stopping and then starting again. When she finished, only a few people applauded.

As Priscilla ran off the stage, Nick's hand felt warm. He looked down at the blue ring. It was glowing in the dim light. For some reason he felt a strong urge to help Priscilla.

He shook the feeling off. Even if he knew what to do, he didn't have time to worry about it now. He was on next.

Mr. McCloskey walked by carrying a music stand. He saw Nick, glanced at his outfit, and shook his head. Then he saw the blue ring and stopped. "Where did you get that?"

Nick shrugged. "It was in the trunk, along with the rest of the stuff."

"Why didn't you tell me about it?"

"I didn't find it till last night. It was inside a crystal. It must have gotten cracked at the Plinski's house."

McCloskey shook his head. "So you decided to open it."

"I was just looking at it," Nick said. "Then it started—"

"To glow," Mr. McCloskey said. "And vibrate."

"Yeah. How did you know that?"

"Let's just say that Harley Davison is the least of your problems right now."

"What do you mean?"

From the stage, Mr. Watkins said, "And now, let's welcome our final act, the Amazing Nicholas!"

"Got to go," Nick said.

He strolled out to the center of the stage. "Ladies and gentlemen! I, the Amazing Nicholas, will now disappear and reappear before your very eyes."

Everyone laughed, as if the only amazing thing would be if he didn't make a complete fool of himself.

Nick grabbed the pocket watch. "Gnosis!" he

yelled with a flourish, and clicked the watch.

The audience gasped. The stage was empty. Nick Herriman had disappeared.

Someone yelled, "Where did he go?"

From the balcony behind them came a voice. "Up here!"

They turned and saw Nick, waving to them with a huge grin on his face. "Aoratos!" he shouted, and disappeared again.

The audience whooped and hollered, craning their necks to see where he'd appear next.

"Over here!" he shouted, popping up in front of the huge picture windows that ran along the left side of the auditorium.

Now every eye was on Nick. "And now, ladies and gentlemen, my most amazing, astonishing feat." He raised his arms in the air, shouted, "Metamorfosi!" and disappeared again.

Laughter and murmurs swept the crowd as they scanned the auditorium searching for him. Then an eighth-grader heard a swooshing sound and looked up. "There he is!"

They looked up and gasped. Nick Herriman was flying in circles over their heads.

They went crazy, cheering and screaming with delight. Nick looked down at the upturned faces, some laughing excitedly, others so astounded their mouths hung open. Harley Davison was dumbfounded. Sarah Williams and her friends stared up at Nick as if he were a movie star. It was definitely the best moment of his life.

Then the back doors to the auditorium burst open.

Fog rolled in through the open doors. A tall figure in a black hat and long dark coat stepped through the fog. He swept off the hat and coat, revealing a robe that shimmered with the colors of a night sky and a hood covering his face in shadows.

The audience gasped. A few laughed nervously, thinking this was part of the act. Others saw the look on Nick's face and knew he hadn't planned this.

The cloaked figure pointed at Nick, a red ring glowing on his outstretched hand. "I am Nocturno," he shouted. "And you have my ring!"

# Chapter 27

The auditorium grew dark, as if a cloud were passing overhead, blocking the sun from the picture windows.

Nick lost altitude instantly. He aimed for the stage, sinking fast and thinking, *Now I get it. The rope only works when the sun is out.*

He landed in a spectacular double-somersault-cannonball crash, hitting his head on the floor and knocking the wind from his lungs.

As he came to, Nocturno stood over him, glaring down. "Give me the ring."

Nick inched away from him. "No."

Nocturno grabbed Nick by the throat, lifting him off the floor. "Foolish mortal. You do not know the power of the ring."

It was a line corny enough to have come right out of a comic book, but Nick didn't think it was a good time to mention that.

Nocturno's eyes were like flames and his breath smelled like burning matches. "If you will not give me the ring, then I will take it."

He held Nick closer and stared into his eyes. The audience screamed, and the room grew darker. Mists swirled around Nick, and he felt himself slipping away, as if he were falling down a long, black hole into the deepest sleep imaginable.

Nocturno slipped the ring off Nick's finger. "Now," he said. "At long last—"

A sound like wind rushed in through the open doors of the auditorium. With his last bit of strength, Nick turned his head. A green blur shot down the aisle toward them.

The next moment, Nick felt himself being grabbed from Nocturno and dropped on the stage. He looked up to see a man in a shiny green uniform standing over him.

"The Meteor!" Nocturno shouted. "You should have stayed retired. You are no match for me!"

"Not so fast, Nocky," the Meteor said. "We'll see who's getting too slow for the job."

Nocturno slipped the blue ring onto his left hand and a bolt of purple lightning flashed between the two rings. "Now my power is complete," he shouted. "Once again, I am master of the night...and the day!"

The Meteor disappeared in a green whirlwind that raced around Nocturno. Green arms shot out from the blur, punching at Nocturno. But a shimmering purple force field emanated from Nocturno's rings, surrounding him and blocking the punches.

"It is over, Meteor!" Nocturno shouted. "Now comes the finale."

He raised his hands. Lightning crackled between the rings and a bolt leaped out, striking the green blur.

The Meteor crashed to the ground. He landed next to Nick, gasping for breath. Nocturno grabbed the Meteor by the neck and lifted him up. "I've waited a long time for this," he snarled.

He peeled back the Meteor's face mask. It was Mr. McCloskey.

The crowd gasped.

"You are finished," Nocturno said, holding Mr. McCloskey by the neck.

Nick ran at Nocturno, pounding at him. "Let him go!"

Nocturno swatted Nick away as if he were a pesky fly. "I will deal with you next, weakling—as soon as I have dispatched this troublemaker."

Mr. McCloskey wheezed at Nick, "K...k...kid..."

What kid? What was he talking about? Whatever it was, Nick didn't have time to figure it out. Mr. McCloskey was growing weaker every second.

Time. Second.

Of course he had time. He pulled out the pocket watch and clicked it.

Time stopped. Nocturno froze. Mr. McCloskey froze. Everyone in the audience froze, their faces petrified in expressions of shock and fear.

Nick tried to concentrate. What was Mr. McCloskey trying to say about a kid? Was it someone in the audience? He scanned the faces, knowing he had to act fast.

Fast.

Of course. Kid Comet.

He ran to the maintenance office, where the gray metal cabinet stood open. He pulled out Kid Comet's uniform. It looked just like the Meteor's costume, except for a thick pair of goggles looped over the hanger. This had to be what Mr. McCloskey was talking about—he wanted Nick to put on Kid Comet's uniform.

It looked too big for him—Kid Comet must have been older than he was—but he stripped down to his underwear and put it on anyway. Instantly, the uniform shrank, just like the shoes had. Now it fit him like a shiny green skin.

He tried on the goggles, worried that he wouldn't be able to see without his glasses. But they fit him perfectly and he could see just fine, as if the goggles had glasses built into them.

Finally, he put on the winged shoes. They molded to his feet also. But these fit better and looked sleeker than the ones he had at home—they had to be a later model. Given the problems he'd had with the other shoes, he figured he'd better try them out before he went back to the auditorium.

He stood up and was about to say the word "run," when he felt a tingling in his feet.

The next thing he knew, he was racing around Mr. McCloskey's office at top speed, creating a mini-cyclone of notes and papers.

He stopped and stared down at the shoes. "Telepathic control," he whispered. Somehow, the shoes were reading his mind and turning on without any voice command.

A chill swept over Nick. He had everything he

needed now. And it was up to him to stop Nocturno and save the lives of everyone in that auditorium.

The uniform had a narrow slit for a pocket. He tucked the pocket watch into it. It was time.

He stepped into the hallway and took off. Two seconds later, he was back at the door of the auditorium.

He pulled out the pocket watch.

"Ready or not," he said. "Here I come."

# Chapter 28

Inside the auditorium, Nocturno held Mr. McCloskey by the neck. "Say good night, Meteor!"

A green tornado raced through a side door and threw itself against the back of Nocturno's knees. "Drop him, you creep!"

Nocturno bellowed with rage and fell to his knees, dropping Mr. McCloskey. "Kid Comet!" he roared.

"That's right, night-breath," Nick said, racing away in a green streak. A moment later, he appeared up in the balcony. "And you'll never catch me."

Nocturno shook his head. "I do not know who you are, but you are no better than the original Kid Comet." He pointed at Nick and fired a purple lightning bolt from the ring. Nick disappeared and the bolt struck the back wall of the balcony.

Nick reappeared downstairs, at the back of the auditorium. "Missed me, Dark Faker."

"Well you may run," Nocturno shouted. "You are a coward, just like the original Kid Comet!"

Nick's ears burned and Nocturno fired again. "Everyone get down!" Nick yelled.

The bolt flashed over the heads of the audience as they screamed and dove for cover.

"Ah, I see," Nocturno said, an evil grin appearing on his face. "Now I know your weakness. You actually care about others."

He fired again. This time, the bolt headed right for the audience.

Nick's mind raced. He needed something to deflect the thunderbolt.

In a split second, he dashed backstage, grabbed the largest cymbal from the band's drum set and ran back to the audience.

To Nick, the lightning bolt seemed to be moving in slow motion, sizzling like a long electric snake. It was headed for Owen Linderman.

Nick poured on the speed. Now the bolt was only inches away from Owen's chest. Nick stretched out his arm with the cymbal. The bolt bounced off it with a dull crack and shot harmlessly up to the ceiling.

"You fool," Nocturno shouted. "Your compassion is a weakness you share with your predecessor."

"Shut up!" Nick yelled, his blood pounding.

"Ah," Nocturno said. "Do I offend you? Is your temper as quick as your feet?"

He aimed a lightning bolt at a dark-haired girl who sat curled into a ball, her legs tucked up beneath her. Nick reached her just before the bolt hit, deflecting it toward the windows.

"Can you stop this?" Nocturno howled. "Or this?" He fired wildly now, aiming lightning bolts at random places into the audience.

Nick sped from row to row, vaulting over chairs, deflecting one bolt, then another. His breath came in great gasps and his muscles ached. He didn't know how much longer he could keep this up. He had to find some way to end it.

Mr. McCloskey gasped, "Look out!"

"Silence!" Nocturno roared, firing a lightning bolt in Mr. McCloskey's direction. Nick blocked the charge and stood over Mr. McCloskey, his chest heaving.

"Don't let him get to you," Mr. McCloskey said. "You can beat him if you control yourself."

Nick stopped. Mr. McCloskey was right. It was time to stop running.

He faced Nocturno. "Here I am, you skunk."

Nocturno emitted a vicious laugh. "I was right," he said darkly. "You are no better than the original Kid Comet. He was a quitter, and you should have followed in his footsteps."

Nick's strength was returning. He glanced at Mr. McCloskey, who nodded. It was a look that said, *You can do it. Do it for Kid Comet.*

"Go on," Nick said to Nocturno calmly. "Give me your best shot."

"Die then, you fool!" Nocturno shouted. He pointed at Nick with both hands and a massive lightning bolt exploded from the rings, crackling and hissing.

Nick waited until the last second. The bolt was almost upon him when he held the cymbal up.

The lightning struck, shaking Nick's whole body, rattling his teeth and making his arms and legs burn like fire. But the bolt bounced off and headed back toward Nocturno.

Nocturno realized what was happening, but it was too late. He turned, twisting to avoid the bolt, but it hit him squarely in the back and sent him flying.

An instant later, Nick stood over him. "I'm not a quitter," he said quietly.

He grabbed an orange electrical cord that lay stretched across the stage and wrapped it around Nocturno's arms and feet.

"The rings!" Mr. McCloskey yelled.

Nocturno twisted, pointing his fingers at Nick, but Nick was too fast for him. He slipped the rings off Nocturno's fingers and tucked them into the pocket of the uniform.

Nocturno howled with rage. "You will pay for this! My power is greater—"

"Put a sock in it, thunder-dolt."

A second later, a dark sock appeared in Nocturno's mouth—just as Tony Chavez realized that one of his socks was missing.

The audience cheered. Kids and teachers wept with joy and relief.

Nick knelt beside Mr. McCloskey. "Are you OK?"

Mr. McCloskey sat up slowly, rubbing his neck and replacing his mask. "I'll be fine." Then, loud enough for the others to hear, he said, "Good work, Kid Comet!"

"Thanks...Meteor."

Mr. McCloskey put a hand on Nick's arm to

steady himself. "You know," he said loudly, "I think it's time we had a talk."

"OK."

"No," Mr. McCloskey said, nodding toward the watch in Nick's pocket. "I mean, I think it's *time* we had a talk."

"Oh, right," Nick said. He pulled the pocket watch out and clicked it. The auditorium fell silent. Nocturno stopped struggling. Once again, time had stopped.

# Chapter 29

"Good," Mr. McCloskey said, still breathing hard. "Now we can talk."

Nick stared at him. "How come you're not frozen like everyone else?"

"Because I was touching you. The watch generates a chronosynclastic field that covers the person holding it and anyone they touch."

"How did you know that?"

"I recognized the watch as soon as I saw it. It belonged to Chronos, the Time Lord. We were in the Heroes League together."

"So you really are the Meteor?"

"I was."

"I thought you were a reporter."

"That was my secret identity. No better job for keeping an eye on crime."

Nick looked around at Nocturno and the immobilized audience. "So what do we do now?"

"First, we need to get rid of those rings."

Nick pulled the rings from his pocket and handed them over. "Where did they come from?"

Mr. McCloskey tucked the rings away. "At one time, Nocturno was a hero named Night Master. The red ring gave him power and the blue ring gave him wisdom and compassion. But he lost the blue ring in a battle with the Ice Man, who wrapped it in that crystal you found in the trunk."

"How did it end up there?"

"I'm not sure. But without the blue ring, Night Master grew ruthless and vengeful. That's when he became a villain and changed his name to Nocturno. Fortunately, without the blue ring he only had half his power, so his evil was limited."

That explained the movie theater heating up, the fog outside the Plinskis' place and the sticky web around Nick's house. "I think he's been after me for a while."

"I don't doubt it," Mr. McCloskey said. "I suspect he never stopped looking for the blue ring to restore his full power."

"But how did he know I had it?"

"He didn't, until you cracked open the crystal. Oh, I think he had a general idea. The rings communicate with each other, so he knew approximately where to look."

That explained the crystal vibrating when he and Tony came out of the movie theater. "How come Nocturno didn't turn into a good guy when he got the blue ring back?"

"It's too late. The red ring warped his personality. Regaining the blue ring restored his full powers, but it couldn't change his evil nature." Mr. McCloskey stood up and dusted himself off. "That's why I need to get rid of these rings."

"What are you going to do with them?"

"Put them where Nocturno will never find them

again." Something told Nick not to ask where that was. "Meanwhile, I have a question for you. What are *you* going to do?"

"About what?"

Mr. McCloskey gestured to audience. "All these people saw everything that just happened. When you restart time, you'll be a hero."

That's right, Nick thought, a grin spreading across his face. He would be a hero.

*The reporters crowded around Nick Herriman, pointing microphones and cameras into his face. "Who is Kid Comet? What can you tell us about him?"*

*"Your guess is as good as mine," Nick said coolly.*

*"Why is it you're never around when Kid Comet appears?"*

*"Just a coincidence, I guess."*

*"What about that magic act? How did you do the disappearing bit?"*

*"Trade secret. Sorry."*

*"Was the flying an optical illusion? Did you do that with mirrors?"*

*"Well—"*

*"Can you explain the sudden rise in your grades this semester?"*

*"Actually, I—"*

*"Is it true that you dumped pudding on the head of everyone in the seventh grade?"*

*"No, that wasn't—"*

*"What makes you think they'll let you keep the trunk?"*

Nick shook his head. "Huh?"

Mr. McCloskey said, "What makes you think

they'll let you keep the trunk, once news of this gets out?"

He hadn't thought about that. With reporters crawling all over, it wouldn't take long for someone to start asking questions about the trunk. If the government found out about it, they'd probably take it away to a secret laboratory to study. And if they didn't take it away, his mother definitely would. His career as a hero would be over.

"Let me ask you something," Mr. McCloskey said. "What does it mean to be a hero? Does it mean having people look up to you? Getting your picture in the paper? Being asked for your autograph?"

Nick shrugged. That was pretty much what he had thought. But now he wasn't so sure.

"Or does it mean doing the right thing at the right time, even if no one else ever knows about it?" He put a hand on Nick's shoulder. "Right now, you have a choice. You can use the trunk to serve your own purposes—and become the superhero with the shortest career on record—or you can stay hidden and use your abilities to help others."

"You mean, like having a secret identity?"

"Sure," Mr. McCloskey said. "You'll be doing good deeds, fighting evil, and righting wrongs. But you'll be doing it secretly."

Nick thought about it for a moment. Maybe Mr. McCloskey was right. Every time he had used the things in the trunk for himself, a disaster happened. Maybe it was time to start helping others. Besides, as a secret identity, Nicholas the Ridiculous, all-around average kid, wasn't bad. People would never suspect that he was a superhero.

"But what about them?" Nick said, pointing to the audience. "Like you said, they saw everything."

"Oh, I'm sure you can think of a way to fix that. In the meantime, why don't you go change?"

Nick sped off and returned a few minutes later wearing his own clothes.

Mr. McCloskey nodded toward the frozen audience. "Did you think of what to do about them?"

"I suppose I could just make them forget everything," Nick said, pointing to the fedora.

"Sounds like a good idea to me."

"Even my magic act?"

"Do you really want people poking around, trying to figure out how you did all that?"

"I guess not," Nick said, sighing heavily. "What about Nocturno?"

"I'll take care of him once you restart time. He won't be any problem without the rings."

"All right." He held up the pocket watch. "Here goes."

# Chapter 30

Nick clicked the watch stem. The crowd came to life again, yelling and cheering. But no one yelled louder than Nocturno, who spat out the sock and roared, "Where are my rings?"

"Come along, Nocky," the Meteor said. "Time to go home."

A moment later, a green wind swept Nocturno up and out of the building.

The crowd cheered even louder. Nick walked to the center of the stage and held up his hands.

"Thank you. Now, if you'll give me your attention, I have an important announcement."

The crowd fell silent.

He pulled the hat down low over his eyes. "Everyone listen to me."

"Listen to you," they all murmured in a daze.

"Good. When I snap my fingers, I want you to forget everything that just happened. Forget about Nocturno, the Meteor, Kid Comet—all of it, beginning with my first disappearance. Are you ready?"

"We're ready," they said.

"OK, then." Nick snapped his fingers.

For a moment, nothing happened. Kids blinked and shook their heads. Nick wasn't sure if it had worked.

He tried to remember what he'd said just before his first disappearance. "Yes indeed. I, the Amazing Nicholas, will now disappear and reappear before your very eyes."

He waited a moment, then whipped the hat off. "Ta-da!"

No one said anything, waiting for the punch line.

"Do you want to see it again?"

They booed. If they'd had rotten tomatoes, they would have thrown them.

"That *is* amazing," Harley Davison yelled. "He turned himself into a nitwit."

"Did you hear the one about the magician who could levitate a rabbit?" Nick said. "It was a hare-raising experience."

Now, the boos were mixed with groans.

"Knock, knock," Nick said.

A few kids shouted, "Who's there?"

"Houdini."

"Houdini who?"

"Houdini do their homework?"

That was enough. They booed him off stage.

"Thank you, thank you very much!" he shouted, walking off stage.

As he stepped into the wings he passed Priscilla Grimes, who stood in a corner crying. It was too bad. She'd been pretty good until Harley ruined her chances. If he had to lose, he would just as soon have lost to her. But there was nothing he could do about it now.

Or was there?

He remembered what Mr. McCloskey had said. Being a hero just means doing the right thing at the right time, even if no one else ever knows about it.

He looked back at the stage. Then he looked at Priscilla again. All right, he'd do it.

He ran out on the stage. Mr. Watkins was talking to the judges as the kids in the audience chattered noisily.

"Excuse me," Nick said loudly.

Everyone looked at him and he ran his fingers along the edge of the hat. "I have another announcement. Please pay attention."

The chatter and laughter evaporated. "Pay attention," they all said.

"Priscilla Grimes is going to perform again. You're all going to forget what happened before."

"Priscilla Grimes is going to perform again. We're all..."

"Right, right," Nick said. "Only this time you're going to listen."

"This time we're going to listen," they murmured.

He ran backstage and called to Priscilla. She looked at him with a worried expression. "What?"

"You're going to sing again."

Her faced relaxed. "I'm going to sing again."

"And you're going to be great, no matter what happens."

"I'm going to be great."

"Now go get 'em."

She turned, walked out on stage and took a deep breath. Then she sang.

"It must have been cold there in my shadow, to never have sunlight on your face."

Her voice soared over the auditorium like a spring breeze. The kids and teachers sat in stunned silence. All except for one.

From the middle of the audience came a noise: "Ook-ook."

Nick stared past the curtain. He couldn't believe it. Harley was such a jerk that even the mind-control hat couldn't make him behave.

"Ook-ook," Harley muttered.

But this time none of his friends joined him. A girl in front of him turned around and said, "Shhhh!"

Priscilla kept singing, a pure, haunting sound that floated over the listeners and fell on them like mist.

"A beautiful face without a name for so long, A beautiful smile to hide the pain."

Harley made gorilla noises again. The people around him told him to shut up.

His mouth fell open. Nobody had ever talked to Harley Davison like that before.

Priscilla kept singing. Her voice was like magic, casting a spell on the audience.

"Did you ever know that you're my hero? You're everything I wish I could be."

For two whole minutes, there were no snickers, no giggles, no papers being thrown. A few of the teachers had tears in their eyes.

Priscilla finished the song, the last note trailing off like a bird sailing toward the horizon.

The audience was silent, and Nick wondered for a moment if they were still in a trance.

Then came the applause. It started like a light rain, then burst into a storm of cheers. They whistled, they stomped, they rose to their feet in a standing ovation. Priscilla tried to leave the stage, but they wouldn't let her go.

Mr. Watkins shouted, "Well, I guess we have a winner."

The judges agreed. Mr. Watkins presented Priscilla a trophy and a check. She stumbled off stage looking dazed, confused, and happier than Nick had ever seen her.

"Congratulations," he said as she passed.

"Thanks." She smiled at him—the first time he'd ever really seen her smile—and despite the freckles and the curly red hair, he recognized that smile.

She stepped out the side door and was instantly surrounded by kids congratulating her.

They swarmed past. Tony caught up with Nick in the hallway. "Man, you really bombed out there."

"Tough crowd," Nick said. "But thanks for your support."

"No problem. Remind me to give you some tips on the finer points of comedy."

"Great. Thanks."

"Mainly, you need new material. I think some of those jokes came from King Tut's tomb."

"OK, OK."

Harley Davison and his posse strutted down the hall. "Hey, Ridiculous," he said, slapping Nick on the back. "I've decided I don't have to kill you after all. You died when you were on stage!" His gang laughed like hyenas and took off.

A group of teachers led by Mr. Watkins passed by. "Clearly, we need to have tryouts next time," he was saying. He glanced at Nick and added, "Some of those acts were...well, embarrassing."

Audrey O'Malley marched by with her group. "That was brilliant," she said to Nick. "But don't quit your day job."

Finally, last but not least, came Sarah Williams and her friends, who just snickered as they walked by.

Tony watched them go, shaking his head. "I guess she's out of the running, party-wise."

"Yeah," Nick said weakly. He stared down the hall at his classmates. None of them knew what he had done. They had no idea he'd saved all their lives, or that he'd let Priscilla win the talent show.

"Are you OK?" Tony asked.

"Sure. I'm fine." He was lying. Maybe he was just exhausted, but his chest was heavy and his eyes were on the verge of leaking. Wouldn't that be the final nail in his popularity coffin?

"Come on," Tony said. "Let's hit the party before all the good food is gone."

"You go ahead," Nick said. "I'll catch up with you later." Right now, he needed to talk to Mr.

McCloskey more than he needed to go to a party.

He waited till Tony was gone and headed for the maintenance office. The door was closed and no one answered when he knocked.

He opened the door and stuck his head in. "Hello?"

Mr. McCloskey lay on the floor, his shirt half-buttoned. The Meteor uniform lay in a pile beside him.

"Mr. McCloskey!" He ran in and knelt beside him.

Mr. McCloskey's eyes creaked open. "My heart..." he said feebly.

"OK, OK," Nick said, trying not to panic. "What should I do?"

"Maybe...call a doctor," Mr. McCloskey said, wincing as if someone had dropped a bowling ball on his chest.

His breathing was shallow, his skin a bluish white. It didn't look as if he had much time.

Nick ran to the closet, pulled out Kid Comet's winged shoes and put them on. "Come on," he said, pulling Mr. McCloskey to a sitting position. "I'm taking you to the hospital."

"Too heavy...for you," he gasped.

"Not a problem," Nick said. He reached around Mr. McCloskey, revealing a bit of purple sleeve beneath the right arm of his jacket.

He hoisted Mr. McCloskey over his shoulder as if he were a large sack of cheese puffs. "Hang on!"

# Chapter 31

Thirty seconds later, Nick deposited Mr. McCloskey on a bench outside the emergency room of Peabody Community Hospital. "I'll be right back."

He returned with a nurse pushing a wheelchair. "Are you a family member?" she asked Nick.

"He's my grandfather," Nick said.

The nurse wheeled Mr. McCloskey in. Within minutes, he was hooked up to monitors, oxygen and an intravenous line. Nick sat in the waiting room till the nurse came to get him.

"He's stable now," she said. "You can visit him for a minute. But don't tire him out."

She left and Mr. McCloskey gazed up at Nick. "Hide my costume," he said hoarsely.

"Sure."

Mr. McCloskey rested a weak hand on Nick's arm. "There's something I...meant to tell you."

"That's OK. Just rest. You can tell me later."

"There may not be time..."

"Sure there will. You'll be fine. Just relax."

Mr. McCloskey sighed, closed his eyes, and went to sleep.

Nick decided this was a good time to hide that costume, before anyone else saw it. He found the nurse and said, "I'll be back later."

"Just a minute." She turned to grab a clipboard. "I

need to get some more information about—"

She turned back and stopped. He had disappeared.

Mr. McCloskey's office was empty, and it didn't look as if anyone had been there. Nick hung the Meteor costume in the cabinet, locked it, and put the key back in the desk drawer.

As he did, he noticed a photograph in the drawer. It was a graduation picture of a young man in a cap and gown. Written across the bottom was an inscription.

*Hal,*
*Thanks for everything. Keep the faith.*
*Run the good race.*
*Paul Herriman*

It was his father. He had given the photo to Mr. McCloskey. They had been friends.

Beneath the photo was a newspaper clipping.

### Peabody Man Killed
### in Hit and Run
Elm City - Peabody resident Paul Herriman was killed late yesterday afternoon, the apparent victim of a hit-and-run accident on Main Street.

A chill ran down his arms. Mr. McCloskey knew

how his father died. Why hadn't he said so?

> Also injured in the incident was Peabody resident Nathan Plinski, owner of a tailor shop near the scene. Plinski, who suffered head injuries, is in stable condition at Peabody Community Hospital. He was unable to provide Elm City police with any information about the accident.

*Mr. Plinski.* He was there when Nick's father died. He'd been injured in the same accident.

Did Mr. Plinski know his father, too? And what was his father doing by the tailor shop that day? Was that just a coincidence?

Only one person would know the answer to those questions, and he wasn't in the habit of telling Nick his secrets.

Nick's gaze fell on the gray cabinet.

Mr. Plinski wouldn't talk to Nick Herriman. But he might talk to Kid Comet.

# Chapter 32

Mr. Plinski sat in a chair by his window, his head nodding. He heard the soft click of the door closing and felt a breeze. He looked up, and Kid Comet stood before him.

"You!" Mr. Plinski said, his eyes opening wide.

"That's right," Nick said, trying to sound heroic. "Kid Comet."

"But you...you're dead."

Nick didn't know the details of Kid Comet's passing, so he decided to avoid that subject. "Do I look dead to you?"

Mr. Plinski put a hand on his chest. "Am *I* dying? Is that why you're here?"

"No, no," Nick said, pulling up a chair. "I just stopped by to visit. And to get your help."

"What kind of help?"

"I'm working on an old case, and I thought you might have some information that could help solve it."

"Of course, of course," Mr. Plinski said. "Anything."

"It's about an accident that took place in front of your shop, several years ago."

"An accident?" He furrowed his eyebrows. "I don't remember—"

"It was a hit-and-run. Please, try to remember. It's

important."

Mr. Plinski stared into Nick's eyes, then down at the floor. "Yes, that's right," he said slowly. "It was an accident."

"Can you tell me what happened?"

"No. I..." He frowned, as if recalling something. "You were there," he said, looking up.

"I was?"

"Yes. It was your old shoes. You wanted them fixed up. A present for someone, you said."

"Oh, that's right," Nick said, though he had no idea what Mr. Plinski was talking about. "Anyway, about the accident—"

"You dropped off the shoes and left, and I went across the street to get a paper."

Nick didn't care about Kid Comet's old shoes. He didn't care about the newspaper. He wanted to know what happened to his father.

"I wasn't paying attention," Mr. Plinski said. "I crossed the street, reading the paper. I didn't see the car."

"And it hit you?" Maybe in the foggy reaches of Mr. Plinski's mind, this *did* have something to do with the accident.

"No," Mr. Plinski said. "You saved me. You pushed me out of the way."

"Was anyone else there?" Nick asked. "A man?"

Mr. Plinski closed his eyes as if it hurt him to think about it. "I don't know."

"Please, try to remember."

"You weren't wearing your costume that day. If you were, it never would have happened."

"What wouldn't have happened?"

"The accident, the accident," Mr. Plinski said, and began to weep. "I'm sorry," he said. "I'm so sorry."

"What are you sorry—"

The door to the room opened and a nurse looked in. "Mr. Plinski?"

A gust of wind blew past and she gathered her sweater about her. "Mr. Plinski, are you all right?"

The old man sat alone, his head in his hands, weeping.

Nick ran back to Mr. McCloskey's office, the thoughts in his head buzzing like hornets in a bottle.

Mr. Plinski had been there when his father died.

Kid Comet had been there.

Kid Comet had saved Mr. Plinski's life.

So why didn't he save my father's life?

Nick ran harder now, his fists clenched, his feet pounding the pavement, more determined than ever to figure out what happened to his father. Whatever it took, he was going to find out.

Back at Mr. McCloskey's office, he peeled off the Kid Comet outfit and tossed it in the closet. He didn't want to wear it anymore, especially since Kid Comet had been there when his father died and hadn't done anything about it.

His father's graduation photo still lay on the desk. The school's information was stamped on the back.

University of New Berkshire
Durham, NB

Where the heck was New Berkshire? Maybe he should have worked harder at geography after all.

He searched through the desk drawers to see if there was an explanation, but didn't find anything. Then he remembered Mr. McCloskey's scrapbook. Maybe something in there would help him.

He flipped through the scrapbook and came to the clipping about Kid Comet. The newspaper image was dark and grainy, Kid Comet's face partly hidden by his mask and goggles. But the hair and eyes looked familiar.

He laid his father's graduation photo next to the clipping. The nose, the smile, the chin—they were all the same.

The realization came in a moment, like a light turning on in a dark room.

His father was Kid Comet.

And Kid Comet hadn't been killed by an alien or a criminal mastermind. He'd been killed by a hit-and-run driver, when he was just being an ordinary, average guy. An average guy who saved Mr. Plinski's life.

Being a hero just means doing the right thing at the right time, even if no one else ever knows about it.

He was always thinking of other people, never

about himself.

Nick fell into the chair, breathing hard as the pieces fell into place.

His father and Mr. McCloskey had been partners.

That explained why Mr. McCloskey had been watching him. Why he hadn't told anyone about the trunk. Why he'd taken such an interest in him.

And now, Mr. McCloskey was sick. Maybe dying.

Nick had lost his father. Now, there was a good chance he was going to lose Mr. McCloskey too.

His head felt heavy. He put it on the desk, the events of the day swirling through his brain.

A minute later, he was sound asleep.

# Chapter 33

Nick woke up. Someone was shaking his shoulder. "Hey," a voice said. "If anyone sleeps in this office, it's me."

Nick's eyes creaked open. It was Mr. McCloskey.

Nick bolted up. "What are you doing here? Are you OK?"

"I'm fine, I'm fine."

"But...I thought you had a heart attack."

"So did I," Mr. McCloskey said sheepishly. "Turns out it was just a pulled muscle in my chest. Guess I'm not as strong as I used to be." He sat down, wincing and bracing his side with one hand. "Of course, it's partly Nocturno's fault. He put on a few pounds over the years."

The scrapbook lay open on the desk, the photograph of Nick's father next to it. Mr. McCloskey said, "Looks as if you've been doing some detective work."

"Yeah. I talked to Mr. Plinski, too."

"And what did you learn?"

Nick hesitated. Now that he had to say it out loud, it seemed crazy. "My father was Kid Comet?"

"Yes," Mr. McCloskey said. "He was."

"But...he was just an average guy."

"Real heroes usually are."

"Why didn't you tell me?"

"I wasn't sure I could trust you. Even after a superhero is gone, his true identity is sacrosanct."

"Sacro-what?"

Mr. McCloskey chuckled, then winced. "Top secret. A secret you don't tell anyone unless you're absolutely, positively sure you can trust them. And I wasn't sure about you."

Nick's face burned. The way he'd been acting, he couldn't blame Mr. McCloskey for not trusting him.

"It's OK," Mr. McCloskey said. "I know I can trust you now. You're starting to act like a hero."

"Yeah, well it hasn't been that much fun so far," Nick said. He told Mr. McCloskey about the nosedive his popularity had taken after the talent show.

"I know, it's not always easy," Mr. McCloskey said. "That's why so many of us had partners, so we'd have someone to talk to. The main thing is not to give up. A real hero doesn't quit."

Nick was quiet for a moment, staring at the pictures of his father. "Why did *he* quit?"

"He didn't quit," Mr. McCloskey said. "He decided there was something more important he wanted to do."

"Like what?"

"Like having a family. You."

Nick's eyes approached leak level again, but he held it in. "He saved Mr. Plinski's life, you know."

Mr. McCloskey looked puzzled. "Who told you that?"

"Mr. Plinski. Well, he didn't exactly tell *me*." He pointed to the cabinet. "He told Kid Comet."

Mr. McCloskey chuckled. "That's brilliant. I always wondered what happened, and Nate couldn't remember anything after the accident."

"He said my dad was dropping off his old shoes. Something about having them fixed up to give to someone."

"Can't you guess who?"

Nick thought about that for a moment. "Me?"

"I think so. He probably wanted to save them until you got old enough. But after the accident, Mr. Plinski must have stuck them in the trunk."

"Wow."

"Why do you think I didn't take those shoes away from you the first time I saw them?"

"I don't know," Nick said. Now that he thought about it, most adults would have taken away something as cool as that.

"The same reason I didn't take the rest of the stuff in the trunk. Because it seemed as if you were meant to have it."

"Tell my mother that," Nick said. Which reminded him. "Does she know about all this?"

"No. Your father never told her. Even though he'd left the business, he didn't think she could handle it."

"I'll say." Her magazines probably didn't have articles on "How to Deal with Those Pesky Supervillains Trying to Even Old Scores."

179

"So your father and I shared the secret," Mr. McCloskey said. "And now it's *our* secret. I guess that makes us partners."

"Yeah?"

"Yes," Mr. McCloskey said, sticking out his hand.

"OK," Nick said as they shook. "But if we're really partners, I have a few questions."

"Go ahead."

"You keep talking about all these superheroes. But where are they? Where did you take Nocturno? He held up his father's graduation photo. "And where's New Berkshire?"

Mr. McCloskey blinked. "What?"

Nick recognized that look—a fake innocent expression his mother used when she knew something but didn't want to admit it. "And while we're at it," Nick said, "where did all these clippings come from?" He flipped through the scrapbook and pointed to a clipping whose dateline read *Boston, Wampanoag.* "Where the heck is that?"

Mr. McCloskey studied Nick for a long time. "Wampanoag is the name of a state," he said finally. "In my world."

Nick stared at him, eyebrows lowered. "What do you mean, in your world?"

"Maybe you want to sit down again."

Nick did.

"Imagine another universe, one very similar to this one, but which occupies a different space-time continuum." He placed his palms together. "They lay side-by-side, nearly identical…"

"You mean a parallel universe?"

Mr. McCloskey looked surprised. Nick said, "I read comic books, remember?"

"Of course. Well, that's where I came from. So did your father."

Nick's heart pounded in his chest. "Does that mean I'm part alien?"

"No," Mr. McCloskey said. "We're humans. We just come from a slightly different version of Earth."

"Different how?"

"There are lots of little things, and a few big ones. Some places have different names. We have a few inventions you don't, and vice versa. Buddy Holly was the president when I left."

"Who?"

McCloskey sighed. "Never mind."

Nick remembered his mother's comment about his father being bad at geography. *He would make the silliest mistakes. Once, he referred to Mexico as Texaco.*

"Of course, the big difference is that superheroes are real there," Mr. McCloskey said. "All the imaginary superheroes in this world have counterparts in that world."

"I don't get it," Nick said.

"I'm not sure how it happened either. Somehow, artists and writers here seem to have picked up ideas from that world without knowing that the things they imagined were real."

Nick rubbed his eyes, trying to make all the pieces

fit. "So how did you get here?"

"There are a few portals between the two universes."

Nick thought about asking where the portals were, but wasn't sure he wanted to know.

"The portals are closely guarded secrets," Mr. McCloskey said. "And they are only used in times of great need."

Nick tried to think of what a time of great need would look like. Mr. McCloskey seemed to know what he was thinking. "Such as getting out of the superhero business."

"What do you mean?"

Mr. McCloskey shrugged. "You can't be a superhero forever. The problem is, superheroes tend to make a lot of enemies, which doesn't make for a very peaceful retirement. So when your father decided to leave the business, I thought he should come here."

That didn't explain what Mr. McCloskey was doing there. "What about you?"

"It was kind of lonely for me after your dad left, and I didn't have anyone to follow in my footsteps. Eventually, I decided to cross over so I could keep an eye on him…and other folks."

He looked at Nick, and now Nick understood something. Mr. McCloskey had also been keeping an eye on *him*. At one time, that thought had made him nervous. Now it felt pretty good.

"Now you'd better get home," Mr. McCloskey

said. "I've got something to do."

As Nick stepped out of the office, Mr. McCloskey opened the metal cabinet and pulled out the Meteor costume. Nick closed the door, wondering what he was up to.

By the time Nick got home, his mother was waiting at the door. "Where have you been? I was starting to get worried about you."

"The chess club had a party, remember?"

She bought it. "Well, how was school?"

He thought for a moment. "Different." Which was definitely true.

Up in his room, he pulled out the list from the trunk and a sheet of blank paper. There was one more riddle he needed to solve.

He copied down the bit of code he'd given Tony, and below it, the translation.

*rsdl rshbjr*
*stem sticks*

He stared at the letters for a minute. Then, without really thinking about it, the answer came.

Of course. Now that he saw it, the code was simple.

He grabbed the pencil and quickly translated the top line of the list.

His eyes grew wide.

This was going to be fun.

Miles away, a man with a grizzly beard and a dirty wool cap pushed a shopping cart down the Main Street of Elm City, searching for deposit bottles. A gust of wind blew past him, rattling newspapers. For a second, the wind seemed to blow open the door to a nearby shop and then close it in an instant.

He rubbed his eyes. Darned things were playing tricks on him again.

But just in case, he pushed his cart to the door and tried the knob. It was locked tight.

Above the door a sign read, "Plinski and Son, Tailors."

With a ragged sleeve, the man cleared a bit of the window and stared in, past dusty counters and empty racks. Dust swirled in the light streaming in from the window. On the floor, a trail of fresh footprints in the dust led to a dark curtain. The curtain had been pushed aside to reveal the back door to the shop. The curtain swung slightly, as if someone had just gone through it.

The man shuffled away, shaking his head. He did not go around to the back of the building. If he had, he might have noticed that the back door to the shop was locked and rusted shut. It had not been opened in years.

And he might have wondered about that.


THE END

## About the Author

Ken Sheldon is the creator of *Sing Along and Learn*, a best-selling series published by Scholastic and used in classrooms across the country. He has written for a variety of publications and served as editor of *Cobblestone*, the award-winning history magazine for children. He contributes regularly to *Yankee Magazine* and performs across New England as Yankee humorist Fred Marple.

Visit Ken's website at *kensheldon.com* or contact him by email to *ken@kensheldon.com*.